Totally Bound Publishing books by Belinda Burke:

Eight Kingdoms
Dark Side of the Sun

I0570749

Eight Kingdoms

DARK SIDE OF THE SUN

BELINDA BURKE

Dark Side of the Sun
ISBN # 978-1-78184-784-8
©Copyright Belinda Burke 2014
Cover Art by Angelique Anderson ©Copyright April 2014
Interior text design by Claire Siemaszkiewicz
Totally Bound Publishing

This is a work of fiction. All characters, places and events are from the author's imagination and should not be confused with fact. Any resemblance to persons, living or dead, events or places is purely coincidental.

All rights reserved. No part of this publication may be reproduced in any material form, whether by printing, photocopying, scanning or otherwise without the written permission of the publisher, Total-E-Bound Publishing.

Applications should be addressed in the first instance, in writing, to Totally Bound Publishing. Unauthorised or restricted acts in relation to this publication may result in civil proceedings and/or criminal prosecution.

The author and illustrator have asserted their respective rights under the Copyright Designs and Patents Acts 1988 (as amended) to be identified as the author of this book and illustrator of the artwork.

Published in 2014 by Totally Bound Publishing, Newland House, The Point, Weaver Road, Lincoln, LN6 3QN, United Kingdom.

No part of this book may be reproduced, scanned, or distributed in any printed or electronic form without permission. Please do not participate in or encourage piracy of copyrighted materials in violation of the authors' rights. Purchase only authorised copies.

Totally Bound Publishing is an imprint of Total-E-Ntwined Limited.

If you purchased this book without a cover you should be aware that this book is stolen property. It was reported as "unsold and destroyed" to the publisher and neither the author nor the publisher has received any payment for this "stripped book".

DARK SIDE OF
THE SUN

Dedication

For a Twin and a Star

Chapter One

This is...one of those dreams.

The Red King scowled in his sleep.

A Samhain dream.

Most often, Macsen's sleep brought him nightmares. He had visions of destruction, of mortals in the woods of the hidden kingdoms, moon and firelight shining on their weapons. He saw flames consuming his palace, or his throne overturned, its frost and darkness both dispelled.

Only on Samhain did Macsen have this dream, in which he was someone other than himself.

He didn't like it. He didn't like not being in control of himself, and while he dreamed Macsen remembered things that he knew would not come back to his memory in waking life.

Other visions, other days...the face of a child, a golden power, and... But it was lost to him then, Macsen's own thoughts caught up in the rush of the images that had hold of him.

Gold grew alive in his hands through some inner power. He looked down, saw a stranger's face reflected in the gilded steel, had a thought that was his own, disassociated with whoever he was in the dream.

Beautiful, he's beautiful. Who are you, stranger?

One hand reached up and pushed back blond hair, but it fell forward again over blue eyes dark as summer twilight.

"My lord—"

Macsen's awareness recoiled.

"—wake up!"

The images wavered like a reflection on a pool.

"Wake up, my lord!"

The vision vanished into darkness. Macsen opened his eyes and tensed his fingers in the fur drawn up over his body. He blinked at the smooth, familiar features of the face leaning over him, then let his hands relax and closed his eyes to the presence of the female bent over his bed. The smile on her face was obscenely cheerful, and all he wanted was to go back to sleep.

For the first time he could remember, Macsen wanted to go back to one of his Samhain dreams. Despite the haze over the recollection, the thought of that male stuck with him, the shade of those blue eyes.

Was he human or *sidhe*? Mortal or immortal? Real...or not? As he considered it, Macsen thought that those blues eyes were set in a face he had seen before. A face he knew, and not from someone he'd drunk. *Sidhe*, then. But who?

A name hovered at the edge of his consciousness.

"My lord—"

The voice cut the thread on which Macsen had been reeling the name into his awareness, and frustration boiled in him.

"Enough, Talaith! I'm awake, go find someone else to torture."

Despite his tone, Talaith's smile didn't change. She obeyed, but without hurrying. Before she left Talaith opened the great window in the western wall to let in the moonlight and the night.

The sounds of his winter kingdom's dances and the horns of the waiting Hunt came faint but clear to Macsen's ears. He felt a tingle on his skin, a cold wind that came through the open window with the scents of pine and snow.

The Red King closed his eyes again and tried to bring back the memory of his fading dream, but as had happened every year before, the details were gone. Macsen remembered only that he had not been himself. That he had seen blue eyes in a beautiful face.

He scowled then, irritated he couldn't remember whose face it was, and threw off the covers. The Red King couldn't ignore his duty, even if he wanted to. The moon was at its half in the sky outside, and tonight was a night of power. His presence was required for the taking of the sacrifice.

But he had seen those blue eyes before, had dreamed of being someone who was not himself before, he knew at least that much. Every year on Samhain night—for how many years now? More than ten? More than twenty?

Macsen wondered if he would ever know what it meant, then shrugged and grinned with all his teeth showing.

Probably. One day.

His was a world in which everything happened for a reason.

Macsen lifted himself out of bed then and crossed to stand naked before the great window that looked out across his kingdom. He tried to push his dream out of his thoughts. It was Samhain, and the night was just begun. He was looking forward to the sacrifice, and wondered which of his pets Talaith had chosen.

He hoped it was one with blue eyes.

* * * *

Macsen passed down a long curving stair and out into the wild celebration of his court. Shouts of welcome and screams of glee greeted him. His presence meant the highest point of the rite had come. With deliberate steps, Macsen passed through the crowd and came to stand at the foot of the stairs that led up to his throne. Talaith was waiting for him, holding a woman spellbound by dark allure.

He took the sacrifice into his arms, stroked her auburn hair and ran his fingers over her skin, pale in the starlight. Her eyes were blue, but not the shade that he was hungry for. Still, Talaith had chosen well as he had known she would. Eight hundred years at his side had taught her his preferences.

Macsen held up the sacrifice before his people and listened to them howl for her death. She was only a human captive from last year's Hunt, but tonight she bore the full attention of the Red Court. Under the pressure of Macsen's allure she submitted to his grasp, to the hungry howl of the *sidhe*. She was a creature without a will of her own.

The Red King put her down on her feet and gathered up the length of her hair in one fist. He addressed his court in a ringing voice.

"For the Hunt, and its power!"

A tide of whispers from his court returned the words to him.

"For the Hunt and its power!"

"Because I am your king, unless one among you would challenge me!"

Below him, a hundred *sidhe* drew a breath in unison. No one spoke. He hadn't thought anyone would. His power was legend, as much to his own as to humans.

Macsen smiled, and bent to open his mouth around the succulent curve of the woman's throat. He penetrated deep with sharp teeth made for this one purpose. A rough groan, some bestial noise, slipped out of Macsen's throat between swallows of red. He drank in the rich flow of blood, endless and all encompassing...until it ended. Then the woman lay still in his arms, but not in languor.

Slowly, enjoying the morsels of flavor, Macsen Cadoc licked his lips and teeth clean of the sacrifice. He dropped her body to the ground and left it. It would be taken care of. Already, small seekers of soft flesh were crawling hungrily out of the crowd toward the fallen body.

Macsen stepped out of the whirling that was the dance as it was reborn, and climbed up to his shadowed throne. Ecstatic taste and energizing sensation wound through him. The living blood he had drunk moved in him, mixed an afterglow like the pleasures of sex with the euphoria of strong wine.

He fell into his high seat and turned his gaze down toward the dancers. There was beauty here no mortal had ever survived, a striving passion beyond all human desire. Over it all, his gleaming winter demesne, Macsen sat enthroned — the Red King. Yet he found that despite the sacrifice, despite the affirmation of his rule, his being hungered for more than just the flow of blood. That desire was the basest of his being, but it wasn't the only thing that moved him...or shouldn't be.

The truth was that he was bored. Ennui had been creeping up on him for years. He had taken the Red Throne in a storm of power when he was only ten years old, but that time was now a thousand years ago. Every day, every decade since had begun to fold into unbroken sameness. He had fought wars and ended them, had drunk the lives of men and women and strange creatures of magic and power. Despite this, or maybe because of it, eternity had grown long for him. Empty. His mind turned on forever, contemplating. He watched the movement of color and light below him, but it was the wind that distracted him from his brooding.

The leaves of the wood overhead shivered and rustled like ancient silk. The land to which he was bound by will and magic shuddered under that wind, a wind that foretold the approach of...something.

In the next moment, Macsen felt that something approaching. What would it be? He scented neither fear nor fire, only purpose, an odor ripe as fresh fruit. What was it? Who did it belong to?

He pushed himself forward on the arms of his throne and looked out across his court. At the very edge of the dancers, he saw a figure move, circling, a figure that did not fit in. Macsen's whole being tingled with watchful alertness, with a sudden and complete awareness of the truth. *Intruder! Trespasser! Stranger, invader, thief!*

A rush of murmurs washed up from the court and the disrupted dancers as many others became aware of the stranger's presence. The smooth, perfect movements became stillness. The pounding of the drums became an equally pounding silence. Many voices reached Macsen's ears, all of them speaking the same thing.

"A woman is here among us!"

"A human woman!"

Macsen stood before his throne and looked down. A hundred shades of mist and silk parted before his eyes and revealed a single figure standing alone. She was indeed human, a fair-haired young woman. She was tall and slender and as she came forward, Macsen saw that she was dressed in worn but well-fitted armor. Her green eyes flashed with a steely edge, and her narrow face spoke only of death.

The intruder's gaze moved around a circle of *sidhe* as the dancers withdrew from the center of the court and surrounded her. Finally she turned so that she was looking up at Macsen and spoke to him.

"You are the Red King?"

Macsen lifted one eyebrow and stared down at her with a gaze that had brought battle hardened men to their knees. It had no effect. She continued to meet his eyes. The lines of her face didn't flicker or change. Death, that was still all he saw in her expression.

Whose death, girl?

"Answer me, creature! Are you the Red King?" Her voice slashed at him.

Creature? Wordless, Macsen nodded.

"Then you are the one I've come to kill. Your life will serve as payment for the lives you and your kind have stolen."

Macsen relaxed in his throne and watched fury play across her face as he did so.

"So you are another huntress."

His voice was light, but his face darkened as she crossed moon-spilled shadows and approached his throne. She was the third huntress to come after him in the last twenty years, but the other two hadn't dared to attack him in his own kingdom.

The huntress came to a halt with one foot on the first step that led up to Macsen's throne. He stared down at her and saw that there was arrogance on her face now, arrogance and anger. Nothing subtle, nothing hidden.

Death. She really means to kill me, the little fool.

The other two women had been older, slower, but more cautious and more knowledgeable, too. They had at least known better than to come after him in his own realm — and on a night of power!

But you couldn't help that, could you, huntress?

The other huntresses had attacked him in the human world, when he was on his own hunt, seeking to salve his selfish thirst. *This* girl, foolish or arrogant, had sought him out in his own place, and tonight was the only night when the veil between worlds was thin enough for humans to pass without a guide...or an abductor.

She spoke at him again, impatient, "Are you going to come down and face me or do you mean for me to kill you where you sit?"

Macsen felt laughter building up in him, but he held it back and shook his head at the invader. "Are you a fool, huntress? Are you so stupid as to think I would accept your challenge when I have nothing to gain from it? Look around you! My whole court stands prepared to attack you at my word!"

His threat stilled her.

"This is not like the battle your ancestors won by accident a thousand years ago, and you are no Amergin!"

The huntress remained motionless, but her gaze darted to the corners of the night, investigating every sound.

"There was no accident! My people won Ireland fairly —"

"Your people won nothing."

Her hand grew tight on the hilt of her sword. Macsen saw her grit her teeth, and leaned forward on the edge of his throne.

"You should know your history. You should know that your ancestors won the lands they live in because of an accident—you should know better than to come here seeking some kind of victory over me."

"No! They won our land because Amergin was stronger—"

"Amergin had the *sidhe's* own power to aid him and the good fortune to be on the right side of someone else's mistake, that's all."

"No—"

"Oh, yes. You mortals think you have the power to use us, to trick us, but you are never aware of what is happening beneath the surface. When the Milesians first came to Ireland, Summer's Queen heard that her husband had made a bet with Amergin over a test of power. The queen thought she would humiliate the king by making him lose to a mere human.

"She was angry with him for taking others to his bed, but she didn't know that it was no bet at stake, but an oath of ownership. A pact that promised the rule of Ireland to the winner."

Macsen shrugged.

"A mistake, as I said. Summer's Queen went to Amergin and gave him the knowledge of how to break her husband's power...and then found herself and all her people subject to her husband's oath. The mortal lands of Ireland were to belong to the Milesians. Summer's people were to stay within their hidden kingdom."

The huntress had gnawed at her lip until it bled, but she couldn't hold back any longer. "No! You lie! It was Amergin's power that—"

Macsen rose from his throne and glared down at her. "It was a mistake, little girl! A single mistake. I know Summer's Queen—vain, intelligent, easy to flatter but hard to please. She was my enemy once, as you are now, and I have taunted her with this truth. Her eyes are the brightest blue when she's infuriated—"

Macsen smirked, then stopped midsentence. Without permission, his thoughts had flashed back to the face in his dream, that precise shade of blue eyes. But no—he put the thought aside. The face in his dream had been male, even if the color was the same.

He shook his head and brought his attention back to the huntress standing in front of him, her face brilliant red as her anger overtook her.

"You are still here? You should have taken that history lesson to heart, girl. You should be fleeing, because I don't make mistakes."

The huntress mounted another stair in defiance.

"Vampire—I will kill you."

Humans had many names for Macsen's kind of being. He was *sidhe*, one of the fae, but the blood-thirst that drove him had named his nature. Vampire. Macsen showed his teeth, taunted her.

"Kill me? You? You are only a little girl interrupting my morning. The rabbit shouldn't seek to slay the wolf—that is not the law of nature."

The circle of *sidhe* that surrounded the huntress tightened without actually moving, but she disregarded the danger of their numerous presences and spoke anyway.

"I didn't come here to listen to you, beast. I came to kill you, I came to avenge the humans you've slaughtered."

She took a step forward and unsheathed her sword. The blade shone with gold. Macsen stared at it, a fine weapon, more so than anything the other huntresses had carried. Even the edge of the blade was gilded, and his dream flashed across his thoughts again.

Those blue eyes — they had been reflected in the blade of a sword like that. He stared hard at it, willing the memory to come back, but his mind filled only with silence.

The sound of other weapons being drawn turned Macsen's eyes away from the huntress' sword. Two of his guards stepped forward — he knew them well, a pair of his favorites. They were siblings, Rhys and Seren, *sidhe* of Macsen's own kind. Their eyes gleamed with killing hunger, and it occurred to him that this trespasser might be good for some entertainment after all.

Macsen spoke in idle tones. "You can't be serious in your threat, little girl. You can't have thought that you could come here and escape, even if you succeeded. The odds are against you. Even if you could slay me, you couldn't kill us all."

"I'm no little girl — my name is Noirine Muirenn, and I'm a Milesian woman. I don't care about escaping, I came prepared to die. As long as I kill you, nothing else matters!"

Macsen allowed a lazy smile to slip across his face. He stepped back and sank onto his throne again.

"Is that so?"

The huntress straightened her back. Macsen saw the knuckles of the hand that gripped her sword go white, but not with fear. *Fury.* He could smell it on her. It amused him, and he turned his attention to the pair waiting by the dais.

"Rhys. Seren. You look ready…"

Seren quivered and reached for him with trembling fingers that came to a halt before they could touch him. Her obvious fervor amused him, as it always did. "My lord— My lord, let me kill her, let me drain the blood from her veins for you—"

Macsen favored her with a smile before he turned to her brother.

"And you, Rhys? Do you share your sister's sentiments?"

A slow grin stretched Rhys' cheeks. "I do—though not her motives. The woman looks delicious, don't be greedy, My King—let me drink her up myself!"

Macsen directed his attention back toward the woman. She still looked fearless, even in the face of Rhys' and Seren's bloodthirsty intentions.

"Little girl, I will make a bargain with you. If you can defeat these two in combat, I'll face you myself. I'll even offer you a prize. One blow, one strike of your blade that I will not dodge or counter…unless you try to take my head off, of course."

Macsen fixed his gaze on her, tasting rage as it rose from her skin in waves of copper odor.

"But you wouldn't do that, would you? To kill me without fighting me—that would be cheap, the coward's way, and you are a warrior, aren't you?"

His tone was mocking but the words were true, or at least she thought so—Macsen could see consternation on her face.

"What is your answer, huntress? Will you try to defeat them so that you might face me?"

Her mouth worked in silence for a moment. Then something changed, something Macsen couldn't identify. Her rage seemed to condense, contract, come close to her and cling to her skin like a second layer of armor. She spoke more quietly than she had before and did not look up at him again.

"Yes. Even though you're offering this because you think I won't succeed, even though you think I'll just be entertainment—I'll do it. To kill you, I'll put up with your mockery a little longer."

* * * *

Macsen wasn't given a chance to answer the huntress' statement. Seren pushed her way forward past Rhys and looked across at the intruder with an expression that conveyed deep disgust.

"You speak so to our king? You dare insult him, when he has offered you such kindness? When he contemplates facing your unworthiness in battle?"

"My unworthiness?"

The huntress' voice rose in pitch and volume for that second word, and Macsen leaned back against his throne to watch.

The girl moved against Seren in a rush. She had been well-trained, that much was obvious, and he drew in a breath that brought him the scent of fury again. Seren wielded a shorter sword than the huntress, but she was taller and her reach compensated for the length of her blade.

Macsen considered Seren. She was known for her sadism, for using her speed and her strength as torment instead of keys to a quick kill. The huntress was only human-fast and human-strong. She might have been able to fight against other *sidhe* of his court, but she was no match for a vampire in a direct contest. Still, she was demonstrating skills that made up for her deficiencies and a will that he found...almost impressive.

The flash of the huntress' sword was a golden arc that deflected the slashing attacks of Seren's blade. She circled Seren warily, but not with fear, and Macsen saw years of practice in her movements. She turned without ever showing her enemy her back, gave ground but allowed no distance to open between herself and her foe. She tested with strikes that probed Seren's defenses — quick, strong, careful.

The sound of sword meeting sword came fast and bright in the air. Macsen sat forward, interested — this girl had talent, he couldn't deny it. He was impressed that she was still keeping up with Seren.

Moonlight slid down the blade of the huntress' sword, provoking Macsen's thoughts again, distracting him from the fight itself. Why gold? It was an uncomfortable metal for his kind, yes, but gold was expensive and humans didn't have the power to awaken the metal — to make it live and breathe in a way that was dangerous.

Macsen saw again in his mind's eye the sheen of gilded steel with a face reflected in it. He remembered the feeling that had overcome him in the dream, the feeling of foreign power, slipping out of him like a stream. Power that stroked the gold, power that coaxed it awake.

The memory made him wonder. Could the woman before him be carrying a weapon like the weapon that had come to life in his dream? Summer's people had the power to do such a thing, but he had been at peace with them for twenty years of mortal time. He had sworn to a pact that would be hard to break, on either side.

More than that, even age-old enemies would not sink so low as to arm humans against their foe. To do so would invite reprisals from every kingdom, so why…did he have that feeling?

Macsen shrugged, dismissed the thoughts from his mind and returned his attention to the fight. While he had been distracted, Seren had landed several blows against the human. The huntress' leather armor showed blood against tanned skin where she had been cut by Seren's blade, but he recognized the pattern of the cuts. Seren was playing, and as the two exchanged a dozen blows in as many seconds, Macsen realized that the huntress knew this.

She was luring Seren closer, allowing herself to be wounded in minor ways. It was a dangerous tactic, but perfect against one as interested in drawing out the play as Seren. Whatever the case, Macsen saw that Seren had profoundly misjudged her opponent. The girl stepped forward and drew close to Seren's body. She turned outward, stepping with her foe—her sword flickered in a curious arc, gold flashing out and back.

The first strike of the huntress' blade cut Seren's shoulder to the bone, and the second laid open the wound, exposed bloody tissue to the air. Seren shrieked, her voice high and thin in her agony. Macsen was surprised, and felt a chill. So much pain, from a human weapon?

His eyes narrowed, and he watched as Seren drew back her arm with a sudden, jerking motion that was still too late. The third flick of the girl's sword severed Seren's left arm just above the wrist. Streaming ichor pulsed from the terrible wound, and this time Seren's howl was piercing enough that Macsen winced at the sound of it. The Red King thought things looked very bad for her, but the next moment changed his mind.

It appeared that the huntress had forgotten about Rhys.

The girl's eyes were on Seren, who stood bent at the waist squeezing the stump of her left arm between her right arm and her body. The girl lifted her sword for a killing blow, aimed to take the head from Seren's shoulders, but at the same moment Rhys ran forward from where he had been watching his sister play. Macsen saw Rhys' sword come up sharply, a swing made wild with rage.

Without turning, the huntress still knew his attack was coming. Macsen detected her knowledge in the tensing of her muscles, the way her whole body snapped to attention and shifted a hair's breadth to the right. Her left hand flashed with a sudden gleam, but her sword was still in her right hand, threatening Seren with its unwavering presence. This was something smaller—a dagger? Yes.

It shone the same bright gold as the blade of her sword, and she used the cross-guard of the dagger to catch the edge of Rhys' sword and turned his blade inward. It was an act Macsen knew required finesse, not strength. Rhys grimaced and tried to use brute force to overpower her, but the girl only smiled.

Macsen saw at once what she was doing. Rhys' own strength would serve as a weapon against him. If he pressed even the smallest bit harder—

Rhys pushed down, his teeth bared, his eyes blank beneath a sheen of crimson fury. The huntress' dagger turned outward, just a little farther, and Rhys' blade changed direction and slid down the gold dagger. The sword moved according to the huntress' will, plunged inexorably toward Rhys' own flesh with all the force he had directed at the girl.

He tried to turn it but could not, and his sword buried itself deep in his thigh. While Rhys gasped and shouted his pain the huntress took the opening she had created and drove her sword through Rhys' chest. She pierced his heart, and the sword jumped in her hand, the last beat of Rhys' body transmitted through the blade. She waited one more moment, then pulled her sword free and struck off his head.

The huntress turned away from Rhys' body and back to Seren, still hunched over her wound and panting. Macsen could see the dark blood pouring from Seren's stump. The flesh that had been cut by the girl's gold blade hadn't begun to regenerate as it should have, but if Seren recognized her danger, she didn't show it. Her eyes blazed, all her previous contempt washed out in rage. In the three hundred years he had known her, Macsen had never seen her like this.

"Rhys! My brother — you killed my brother — "

"Oh? Aren't you more worried about your hand?"

The huntress' voice was cool and mocking, but Seren's was not. Not anymore.

"I only need one hand to take out a bitch like you."

The sword Seren gripped in her right hand wavered despite the venom in her words. Macsen saw the point slip as her gaze caught on her brother's body. She staggered, and Macsen wondered how long it had been since Seren had hunted, wondered if there was some other reason her wound wasn't healing. That sword —

The woman feinted, and Seren responded wrongly. The golden dagger slipped up under her defenses and slashed her throat open, but it was not an immediately fatal wound as it would have been for a human. Macsen had time to see Seren's eyes open wide with surprise before the huntress turned and a single backhanded slash of her sword took Seren's head from her shoulders. Both of them, brother and sister, beheaded — was it because Macsen had mocked the huntress with a free blow?

Seren's body slumped where it stood and fell forward, painting the grass with blood.

Macsen stood compulsively as Seren fell, then forced himself to nonchalance as he made his way down the stairs from his throne. He felt, not remorse, but slight regret. Seren had been devoted, and Rhys dutiful. The price of his entertainment had proved high, and the deeper frustration that had been awakened by his dream was not appeased. The trespasser's presence was no longer amusing, and now he was insulted. Angry, and insulted. What to do?

He wanted to teach her another lesson, a lesson about what it meant to challenge him in his own land.

"Well done, little girl. Are you ready to take your prize?"

"Enough of your mocking, vampire. Stand and face me — no more stories, no more lies, no one else between us — "

Macsen stopped on the very last step, balancing on his back foot, then flung himself forward. In a moment he stood still in front of her and grinned. The woman leaped back three steps and crouched, readying sword and dagger.

"Did you forget, huntress? I offered you the chance to wound me if you won and I always keep my word. Come, see how you fare against me, against the strongest of us...but be wary, girl. The difference in power between me and such as Rhys and his sister is more than you know."

"No — the battle will be fair between us. I've no fear of you, creature!"

She spat the words at him and Macsen gained a dangerous expression. "You would refuse me?"

There was only arrogance on the girl's face, magnified by her victory over Seren and Rhys. Didn't she know that the way they had underestimated her had killed them as much as she had? Idiot girl!

In a movement so quick that he was not a blur, but moving light, Macsen darted behind her. He slipped his right hand around her waist, grasped her chin with his left hand and tilted her head to one side. He snapped at her with wicked teeth, thirty gleaming pearls sharp as daggers beside her throat, and delighted in the fear finally visible on her face.

Macsen scented the shining vein beneath her skin, the throbbing jugular that tempted him — then, as he had expected, he felt pain across his unguarded chest when the huntress remembered the weapons in her hands and slashed at him.

The dagger penetrated deep and burned faintly, uncomfortable but not the roar of pain he had expected. Macsen felt the energy of the weapon, the living presence of the awakened gold, and leaped backwards a full step in the same moment. He expected the pain to linger, for that dangerous energy to weaken him as it had Seren. He was surprised when there was nothing but that vague discomfort. It dissipated almost immediately and a deep, healing itch settled into the wound. Why it wasn't burning him was a mystery, but that gnawed at him less than the fact that this huntress, this trespasser, had tried to wound him with *sidhe* gold.

The agreement between the hidden kingdoms, unbroken since the beginning of time, had been broken. The proof was the weapon that hummed in this huntress' hands!

This close to her he could feel it, a straining sunlight power. The arrogance of her! The ego of her act! Coming here, wielding such a weapon — her audacity stunned him. He opened his arms and let the girl fall free.

She stumbled, then turned and caught him across the side with the edge of her sword. The blade cut deep. Dark blood poured out around it and Macsen let out a hiss of pain, but once again the gold failed to hurt him as it should.

The huntress smiled at him. She looked pleased with herself.

With a casual gesture, he pulled his bloody tunic over his head and cast it aside. He reached out and took hold of the blade of her sword, though she struggled and it cut him. He jerked the girl forward with his grip on the blade, and when she stumbled this time Macsen snatched at her arm and crushed her wrist in his grasp.

The huntress screamed and her fingers opened. The sword dropped from her hand. She slashed at his body with the golden dagger, but Macsen ignored it and didn't let go.

"The weapons — who made you those weapons, little girl?"

He squeezed his fingers tighter, and took satisfaction in the sharp snap of the fragile bones in her wrist. He took more in her wail, high and thin and lovely.

"Are you going to answer me? Are you going to tell me how you found one of us with the power to make such blades?"

Her eyes opened wide.

"One of you—Rud's not one of you, he's one of Summer's people! Dealla said it, it must be so—"

Macsen stared at the huntress, her mouth open and panting with the agony of her crushed bones, the white sclera visible against the wide darkness of her eyes. Whatever she saw in his face in that moment, it pushed her to new depths of desperation. He saw the moment when she broke, when fear or fury or both impelled her to strike at him again with the dagger she still held in her left hand. Once, twice she slashed at him. Then Macsen reached out with his other hand and caught her by the throat.

She was brave, he had to give her that, but as he tightened his fingers around her throat the girl went still. Perhaps she listened finally to ancient instincts— he felt her grow motionless and quiet in his grasp. Her pulse fluttered like a rabbit's beneath his thumb, and Macsen slipped his thumbnail across the skin of her throat. Diamond-sharp, it sliced into her flesh, but not deeply. It was just enough that the steaming odor of her blood slipped into the air again with the red stream that came from the wound.

Macsen bent and dragged his tongue across the trickle of red on her skin before it could reach the collar of her tunic. Her blood was bitter hate, sweetened by the thin sugar of fear.

"Delicious."

It was then that the huntress found the strength to face the pain of his grasp, the strength to struggle against the death that her own good sense must be telling her had come for her. She struggled with the gasping strength of all life in its last moments, but that wasn't enough. Macsen held her arms apart and leaned close to her ear. He spoke words that he knew she would hate to hear—words he knew she wouldn't be able to deny because they were true.

"Against my guards you did quite well, but you are a thousand years too early to challenge me. You think yourself righteous, but I hunt to survive. So do all my kin, my court, while you came here with no such need! Little girl…"

Macsen brought the heat of his breath against the curve of her ear and felt her shudder.

"You wanted to save humans, to avenge your kin? I will drink them all, even the one who made your weapons—the son of Summer with the beautiful blue eyes."

He heard her draw in a shocked and terrible breath, a breath that told him his suspicion, his inference, was the truth. The dream was real!

He sank his teeth into the curve of her throat.

Macsen sucked at the wound his fangs had made in her flesh and tasted the spurting freshness of venous blood for the second time that day. A crimson well came up again and again from her throat.

When the surge had become a trickle, he backed away, satisfied—for now.

The girl's eyelids flickered at him. Her pupils were wide and sightless, and Macsen saw dim consciousness struggling there in vain.

"You are dead now, little girl. I will send your bones to your kin, and maybe they will learn from them."

Her chest heaved with the effort of drawing in even a single breath, and still she answered him.

"I am…not a…little girl! I am…Noirine…Muirenn. I…am a woman…of the Milesians…"

Pain erupted in Macsen's left thigh and dragged downward. He shouted and dropped the girl, surprised.

The huntress had never let go of her dagger. He had underestimated her after all. Macsen pulled the gold-bright blade from his thigh and scowled. Then, slowly, he smirked.

"A little pain is worth it for proof that my dream was real. What was that name she said — Rud?"

Macsen scowled. Rud was a word that meant thing, not a name for a person. What did that mean? What *sidhe* would accept such a name? What *sidhe* would forge weapons for mortals to use in defiance of the ancient agreement? It was a question that needed answering — and soon.

But not tonight.

The huntress had interrupted, but in the mortal world it was still Samhain night and time for the Wild Hunt to ride. Macsen turned and faced his court then and saw them chafing to be free. They had watched enough blood spilled tonight. Now they were eager to spill some of their own.

"It is time. It is time for the Hunt!"

A howl went up from the *sidhe* of the Red Court, vampires and shadows, *dullahan* and banshee, blind crows and hollow specters. Macsen led them streaming through the forest and across the river — out through the great barrow and into the mortal night. Anglesey was empty, and Ireland was forbidden to many, but Wales called to them, Wales and the whole of Britain.

When morning came to the world, the Wild Hunt descended back into the hidden kingdom. Macsen took what was left of the girl's body to the edge of the wood and set flame to it.

When the embers were cool, and the mortal night had come again, Macsen slipped out of his own kingdom a second time. He brought the huntress' bones wrapped in leather, and passed through the barrow with murder and mischief mingled in his mind. He would pay a visit to the kin of this huntress — he would send them her bones, and take blood in return.

"And that *sidhe* — the one that girl said was of Summer's people — Rud. His life will be mine, too."

Chapter Two

Black...
Bang!
Bones.
Clang!

Bran Fionnan flexed his arm a few times, rubbed the muscles and set down his hammer. The rhythms of pulling out the gold wire and shaping the gleaming spirals had never failed to dull the throbbing in Bran's chest and in his head — until today. Today, even the ringing of his hammer wasn't enough to drown out his thoughts.

Early this morning, he had received the burned and blackened bones of Noirine Muirenn. This afternoon had been her funeral, and Bran's thoughts and feelings roiled with confusion and turmoil. Some few of her living relatives and companions still lingered in the house that was now his alone — if only by default. They were drinking and talking, but they weren't concerned with him, and Bran had taken the first opportunity he had to escape their company and go back to his work.

Now that he had retreated to the smithy, he found himself unable to concentrate on anything.

Steam dewed Bran's eyelashes like tears, and he blinked them away impatiently. Noirine had been the natural daughter of the couple who had raised him—his *sister*, or so he had called her in his youth. Bran pushed aside the sheet of gold he had been hammering and turned his back to the fire, leaned against the raised stone lip of the forge. He ran the backs of his hands across his face, his forehead, ran his fingers through his hair.

He felt hot inside and out. The heat of the metal, the forge, the fire—it was tangled together with the burning of a deep anger. There had been no love lost between himself and his sister. The day she had become a huntress, any closeness that had existed between them had vanished.

"Just because I'm *sidhe* — as if that mattered!"

He knew the words were a lie as soon as he said them. Of course it mattered, how could it not? To be *sidhe* was to be inhuman. To be a monster—or so she'd thought, anyway. She hadn't been the only one. Bran had been angry with Noirine for many years, but now she was dead. Now, his anger was focused on his own life, not on her. The truth of his existence had been brought more sharply into focus by her mortality. With her dead, there wouldn't even be periodic arguments to look forward to. There was nothing left but for him to be used by the people who had *stolen* him until he died. His last link with the mother who had raised him, the only mother he truly remembered, was severed now. What did he have to sustain him? His work?

Bran eyed the gold gleaming by the forge over his shoulder and scowled.

His work was the price of his life, and nothing else. He didn't even possess his own name — he was Bran Fionnan, but the Milesians only called him *Rud*. *Rud* — thing. Not a person, not a life, not someone with meaning even if he had purpose.

The tapestry of Bran's life had been irreparably torn when he had been stolen from the place where he belonged, and after so many years, the threads were shredded and knotted with pain.

It was only in his dimmest, earliest memories that he heard a woman's voice saying his name, pale lips moving in a golden face. *Bran, my shining Bran Fionnan*. He had wondered many times if the golden woman was his mother, but he didn't think he would ever find out. His memories of his life *before* were almost nonexistent.

Despite that, he would never forget being taken away. That first panic, so intense it had blanked out all thought. Just thinking of it now he could feel it again, something cold closing around his heart — no, he would never forget that. Hands had grabbed at him, then covered his mouth. He had heard hushed voices, rough and guttural, and he had felt rope that chafed and stung. Then had come a blow to the head — and pain — and darkness.

Bran had woken to find that the place full of light he had known since his earliest memory was gone. Instead there was the mortal night, and a house, a house the top of the hill that overlooked the Milesian king's palace.

This house.

The memory was agony, and Bran turned his thoughts back to the morning's events. The leather wrapped parcel of Noirine's bones. The promise of an empty future —

Bran crossed to his work table then, turned his attention to a staff on which the gold-work was just begun. His fingers moved idly over smooth, gilt inlay in triskelion shape, the most sacred of the sacred spirals. He shook his head to clear it, then pulled a square of leather piled with gold wire toward him and began to work.

He followed the carved surface of the staff, reaching for the sunlit power that slept within him and laying it down with the gold. He muttered to himself as he worked, ignored the heat of the fire at his back and bent closer to the end of the staff he was working on.

"Didn't have to die—whole thing's pointless, anyway. Not just me that suffers from Milesian pride...not that it does me any good to share the suffering. They'll keep asking for weapons and sending women off..."

Bran dashed sweat-dampness from his face with the back of his arm and scowled down at the wire in his hand. It was pure, fine gold, but it wasn't what had his attention.

"Noirine won't be the last, just like mother wasn't."

A smiling face flashed into his mind. The woman hadn't really been his mother, but she had treated him like her son anyway. She had been the only one who had seen him as a child, and not a monster. Even the first day, she had been a soothing presence to him, soft white hands that had washed away the black terror of being stolen.

She had been the only one to treat him like a person and not a tool, to offer him love or at least the semblance of it, to keep him beside her, to touch him, to hug him, to make him part of the human world. For her, if not for the father or the sister who were part of his adopted family, he had soft feelings.

Of her, too, there were now only black bones and memory left. Bran's love for his sister had long been buried beneath anger, beneath the rage that was the core of his being. His mother...her, he still missed. She hadn't been the one to steal him, only the one to raise him, and she had done the best she could. Still—he did not owe her for her care. He refused to owe any Milesian anything.

Old doubts strove for the surface of his thoughts then. If she had really loved him, wouldn't she have brought him back to his own kind? If she had really loved him, wouldn't she have told him how to get home?

Unless she didn't know.

Thoughts of her, warm in memory, warred with the anger, narrowed Bran's eyes and tightened his lips to a thin line. His own kind—thanks to these people, he barely knew what that meant.

The anger that drove him came from the circumstances of his life. He had always known he was different, it had been obvious even from the beginning. He remembered a brighter world, though barely, and being afraid of the night because he had never seen it before. He remembered the first time he had touched his power and glowed gold with it, but even then he hadn't known why he was different. Not until Noirine had gone to begin her training.

She had come back from her first meeting with the Council as a huntress' apprentice and looked at him with cold and fearless eyes. She had spoken to him with the cruel honesty of childhood, and with only a few sentences she had broken apart his world with the truth he had always known but never recognized.

Now, while he brooded on it, her words and their childish tone repeated themselves in his consciousness.

"You're just a sidhe, Rud! The Clan took you when you were a baby, to help us fight. You're not my brother! You're not even human, and if you aren't good, I'm to kill you!"

Shortly after that he had begun to learn his work, to learn that he could wake something in the yellow metal that his teachers brought him. He learned to touch the power he had discovered within him to the gold's own sleeping essence, like touching a spark to a pool of oil. He grew quickly, more quickly than other children his age, and as he grew, so grew the gleam in his eyes, the strength in his slender limbs and a passionate fondness for the woods and the wilderness.

In secret, when he could, he had looked for the barrows that might be able to lead him to the hidden realms where the *sidhe* lived. They must be there, because the Milesians had taken him, but he had never found a way.

Each time, he had been forced to return back to this house, back to the work and the loneliness that was waiting for him...

Bran let out a slow, heavy breath and tried to shake off the weight of his thoughts. He stretched his hands and rolled his shoulders, reached up to rub at a momentary ache in his neck then bent over the weapon again.

Spirals flowed from beneath Bran's nimble fingers and took shape on the surface of the staff. It was to go to some girl he was sure would grow cold and die because of it—and he, the maker of the weapon, would carry part of the responsibility for her lost life as long as he existed.

"Some little girl—some little girl, should be playing with dolls—she'll get a weapon instead."

He had scowled to himself when he had received the order for this staff, but he had known better than to refuse. Bran had only tried to refuse the orders of the king and his council once. Bran still bore scars that spoke to that encounter, could still hear the echo of the king's voice beating at him. *Traitor! Obey, or die!*

As if the memory was a signal, Bran heard real voices. The visitors whose speech had been a dull hum heard through the walls of house and smithy grew momentarily louder as they stepped outside, passed the door of the smithy and turned toward the road. The sound tapered off as it receded, and the silence that followed on its heels was thick and dull and all-encompassing. Not a one had thought to do so much as call out goodbye.

Bran thought it was probably better that way. Better for them to ignore him as much as possible—better for them to pretend he didn't exist. It was how he had stayed alive for so long, he thought—that pretending. The Milesians had an easy facility for silence in his presence. They came for him only when they had some new task for him, some new weapon to forge.

His eyes on the staff he had been working on, Bran wondered if the sword and dagger he had made for Noirine had helped her give a good account of herself—but then, if they had, she would have come back alive. Noirine had known the weaknesses and strengths of the one she had been tasked with killing. She had known the risks, had pushed forward regardless. To do her duty. To suffer her doom.

"To kill the Red King. To end the Wild Hunt he leads. Why'd she go, anyway? Let the Welsh take care of their *sidhe* if they want to. Let them sacrifice their women! I wonder, though..."

A crack of thunder echoed outside.

"I wonder...if the Red King is like me? I'm not a vampire, but I'm still one of the *sidhe*. I wonder if that makes us the same?"

Bran banished the thought. Lingering on things like that would drive him mad. Sweat had beaded on his brow and he let out a sigh and wiped it away with the back of his arm. Rain beat loud and sudden on the low turf roof over his head, and in the heat of the forge it was a mocking sound. Bran ignored it and kept his attention on the gold.

Time passed. Over and over Bran softened the wire, finessed the smooth inlay. Within him an endless well of power rose to the work, waking the gold to a radiant energy reminiscent of the sun at noon. When he was through, Bran laid the staff aside carefully. He was pleased with the finished product if not its purpose, and it was with a feeling of achievement that he stepped outside, away from the fires and the heat. He dunked his head directly into the barrel of water that sat by the door and came up gasping, blinking water off his lashes. His thick blond hair was soaked dark and dripped onto his shoulders, but the water felt good on his bare skin. It made him wish it was still raining, but the heavy downpour he had heard while he was working had faded to a damp mist that did him no good.

There was a bucket on the ground beside the barrel, and Bran stripped out of the trousers and heavy apron he wore while he worked and used the bucket to pour water over his body. *Cold.* Delicious. It stripped the salt and sweat from his skin and washed away even the memory of the forge's heat.

Bran breathed deeply, shook his hair back out of his eyes then froze.

"Bran Fionnan…"

The whisper of his name—his actual name—came out of the dark with no source and held him still for an entire minute. The guests were gone, and none of them knew that name. Even if they had, none of them would have used it to address him.

"Hello? Someone there?"

He peered into the dark and saw nothing. There was no other sound, no response, and Bran shrugged and poured another bucketful of cold water over his body. He shivered in the breeze that had come with the storm, then put the bucket down and dried his hands on his discarded apron.

There was still nothing to explain where his name had come from—had he only imagined it?

With a shrug and a sigh, Bran sat on the ground and relaxed against the wall beside the barrel. He let his head fall back with a faint *thunk*, and savored the faint chill of the air as it moved over his naked skin.

* * * *

Macsen carried the bones of the huntress across the narrow sea that divided the coast of Britain from Ireland. Summer's people might be barred from the green isle, but nothing prevented Macsen from crossing the water and going where he pleased.

When he reached the coast, a handful of silver and careful speech gained him a messenger who knew enough to bring the bones of a huntress to her kin. Macsen heard the name of his intended prey then for a second time. Murmurs and rumors were everywhere, and the man he had chosen offered useful information for more silver. The dead huntress was known, both her name and her occupation, and so was the name of her only surviving kin. There was talk of her brother and that name, *Rud*, which he already knew, was spoken in a guarded whisper that Macsen heard with some confusion. The huntress had said that Rud was one of Summer's people, so how could he also be her brother?

The messenger left as soon as Macsen turned away from him, and began to make his way from the coast along the river. Macsen followed him across the landscape slowly. He was grateful for the twilight, but he could travel only as fast as the one he was following, and the man was in no hurry.

The night had passed by the time he came near the palace and the village that surrounded it. Macsen kept back, observing, but the messenger didn't stop for long. He asked a few questions and received more than a few odd looks, but went straight following a narrow dirt road along the riverbank and up a short hill. Only a single house stood there, far from everything else. The sun was barely risen, but smoke and steam rose from a low, narrow building attached to the house. The door opened, and the messenger stepped close and handed in his burden, but there was no outcry of grief and no one came out of the house.

Macsen frowned and watched from a distance as the messenger took instruction from someone inside and left, moving quickly now—but that no longer mattered. Macsen had no more use for him.

He contemplated going forward and bursting into the house, but he could feel dangerous energies even at this distance. Gold, living gold…a great deal of it, too. The weapons that the huntress had wielded against him hadn't caused him any trouble, but he had seen their effect on Seren...and on Rhys. He was unwilling to risk himself just because he was impatient.

Macsen stayed near, a shadow of watchful malice that hid in the shade of the trees. The sun passed high overhead and he saw men, women and children make their way from the village to this lone house at the outskirts. At first he was aggravated by the number of strangers. How would Macsen know the one he was looking for if he had never seen him before?

Everything became clear to him in the first instant Macsen's gaze fell on this Rud. He knew why the voices had been hushed and cautious. Even at a distance, even in a crowd, he could tell that the one he was focused on was the right one. He could feel power sparking in response to the sun overhead, he could tell that the one he was watching was not human.

Macsen moved closer, still unseen, readying himself for violence, letting loose his hunger. He breathed deeply, and in that moment he was caught.

He could have massacred them all, Milesians and one gleaming *sidhe*, but the scent of the gleaming youth before him was crushed sunlight and sapphire that Macsen's hunting senses drank deeply in. It was familiar and it captivated him. Macsen was confused, curious. He took a step forward, entranced, then held himself back and melted back among the trees.

Late in the afternoon, most of the visitors and strangers left and the one Macsen had his eye on went back inside with the few that remained.

Steam and smoke began to issue from the forge again, and Macsen smiled to himself and watched the sky, waiting for darkness. The sun didn't hurt him, but it was an aggravation he didn't want to deal with if he didn't have to.

When night fell, Macsen made his way closer a little at a time. As the darkness increased so did his strength, his senses, his perceptions. Something uneasy tingled at the edge of his awareness, but he wasn't sure if it was the gold he had felt earlier, pulsing at him, or something different entirely. Power, definitely power...but he couldn't focus on it, couldn't locate or identify it and that bothered him.

Malice. That was all. Watchful malice —

But then Macsen was distracted utterly by the one he had been watching, by a beauty of form that matched the scent that had snared him. More-than-mortal sight caressed every gleaming inch of his prey's body as Macsen watched him strip out of heavy, dark clothes.

He stared as the youth poured water over his skin, skin made gold by the sun and carrying shadow in the indentions of smooth muscles sharply defined. He was neither tall nor short, perhaps five feet and nine inches, perfectly poised even dripping with cold water. He had a lean, toned look that Macsen loved in his men, and when he finally turned so that he was facing in Macsen's direction, the blue of his eyes was sharply visible even in the dimness, a shade that hesitated between cobalt and zaffre.

Twin bolts of lust and elation flushed through Macsen and stunned him to silence. Those eyes — those eyes! He slipped forward across the grass, still in the shadow of the trees that grew at the edge of the hill, and stared at the face before him. Like the eyes, he knew that face — angles and planes rounded with the last stroke of youth, that nose, straight and narrow — those full lips, parted now to let out a heavy breath.

The dream was real! In a single, rapturous moment a flood of images came back to Macsen, dreams and memories that had been sleeping in his mind.

This was the one. This one, he remembered everything now, everything from the beginning. He remembered the very first dreams of a child with the curve of his cheekbones bruised and purpled, visible in a watery reflection, and he remembered something that had come before any dream, something from his waking life.

"Bran Fionnan."

Macsen's thoughts raced, aligning suspicion and memory. Twenty-three years ago, he had signed a treaty of peace and good intentions with Summer's Queen and her people. Twenty-three years ago, he had given his oath and exchanged the blood of the bond, not with the queen, but with her young son, Bran Fionnan — a golden child, only four years old, blue-eyed and beautiful as his mother.

Macsen had sworn an oath that promised mutual trust and fidelity, had sworn never to harm and to aid when he could. The queen had demanded such a promise, so that her son would be safe even if the peace unraveled, but her insistence hadn't mattered in the end.

It was humans who had caused trouble. Humans who, after a thousand years of separation between Summer's people and the mortal world, had stolen Summer's prince. Not even the queen had been able to discover who had taken her son, or to where...and now Macsen had found him.

The dreams showed him the progression from the golden child he had met in Summer's kingdom to this gorgeous youth. *Bran Fionnan.* Yes. It was him, there was no doubt about it.

Macsen felt a charge of excitement. What to do, now that he knew that the humans responsible for a most terrible theft were the same humans who so aggravated him? What to do now that he had found this stolen prince? He had come to destroy the one called Rud. He had come to avenge the agreement that he'd thought had been broken and to put an end to the Milesian threat, but it was clear to him now that the one he had come hunting was not a traitor but a victim. A stolen child, kept captive here among these humans —

Macsen knew Bran's world from Bran's perspective, knew his loneliness, his guilty fear, the way he had been treated by those around him. That knowledge woke a burning hunger for revenge.

Without being told, Macsen knew what had happened, could even guess at why. The Milesians, tasked with slaying him and with ending the Wild Hunt, must have been aware even at the beginning that no mortal power would be enough to fight him.

They had trespassed on ancient oaths for the sake of mercenary greed, for the sake of ancient hatred — had stolen a child of Summer to forge weapons that would be of use to them. It had probably been chance that Bran Fionnan had been the one they stole, but that didn't matter. The thought of a *sidhe*, even one of his old enemies, being used by humans grated within him.

There would be time for vengeance, but for now, he put his thoughts away. His priorities were changing the longer his eyes lingered on naked skin in the moonlight.

Macsen watched as Bran reached for the bucket a second time and poured it over himself. He stared, hungry, and felt his first flush of desire return. The muscles in those lovely arms tensed and flexed beneath his skin. The water sluiced down his back, over buttocks and thighs, over his chest and flaccid maleness and down the strong length of his legs. Drops remained, glistening, on the sparse down on his chest and on the darker blond of his pubic hair.

Macsen leached every detail from the scene and only came forward when Bran was settled against the wall.

He muted the glare of his inhuman presence and stepped out of the shadow and into the moonlight. He saw instant wariness come to life in those blue eyes as they were opened, but no recognition. So this stolen prince didn't know who Macsen was.

Interesting.

Now that he had found Bran, the oath Macsen had taken meant that he would have to help if he could. The thought occurred to him that Summer's Queen would be possessive, and unlikely to want to share her son even with the one who had rescued him. Macsen found that this was not a thought that he liked, and considered ways around it.

Bran said nothing as Macsen approached him, and Macsen could think of only one thing to say, the thing that was most on his mind.

"So beautiful...or do you prefer handsome?"

The one in question only stared for a moment, obviously confused by such an approach. Macsen reminded himself that he was just a stranger—and that Bran wouldn't be used to strangers who stared at him like he was a precious treasure. Still, Macsen couldn't help dragging his gaze over his find as he stood.

Bran moved his arms back and clasped his hands behind his head, stretching. The muscles of his triceps and biceps stood out strongly, but Macsen's eyes were drawn lower, to the elongated torso, the deep V of his pelvis and the hint of arousal standing out now from pubic curls. Arousal—did Bran like to be looked at? To be *appreciated*?

Macsen smirked to himself.

He could make use of that.

* * * *

Bran ran his hands back through the shaggy wetness of his hair. He only considered getting dressed for a moment. The stranger had already seen him, and the sweat-stained clothes and heavy apron he had been wearing would stick to his skin and chafe him. It was late, and he was used to being inconvenienced for the sake of anyone else. That didn't mean he was going to be uncomfortable, too. He was wary of trouble, but one man alone wouldn't dare come to confront him, and though the stranger's face was invisible to him in the darkness, the voice was unfamiliar enough that Bran was sure this wasn't someone he'd ever met.

"They call me Rud, stranger. Did they send you up from the village?"

The stranger shook his head and the movement showed Bran brilliant, violet eyes that held him motionless. Dark presence rose around him, almost tangible.

"No. No, I was not sent from the village—and you aren't Rud, even if that's what these fools call you."

Bran narrowed his eyes and a shiver passed over him, a prickling of...something at the back of his mind. The violet eyes gleamed at him, bright and focused. The stranger's voice licked at him, and the words that came next fell like weights and pinned him.

"We have met before, Bran Fionnan."

A tingle raced up his spine. He met the gaze of the piercing eyes still fixed on him and felt another shudder crawl across his skin. *My name!* When Bran finally gathered his thoughts enough to speak, his voice was harsh with confusion. He meant his words to be strong, challenging, but instead they came out low and almost strangled in his throat.

"You! How do you know that name?"

His visitor took a step forward. "Because we have met before."

The stranger took another step, then another, and another, and Bran backed up without thinking, shook his head in denial even as he moved backwards.

"No—no, I'd remember it, I know I would—"

But he hesitated, because those eyes...was there a word for something that was familiar even as it was not? Something brushed Bran's consciousness, his memory. Was it the shadow of a dream he couldn't remember, or the shadow of a dream he had never had?

The stranger smiled, showing no teeth, and stepped forward again. Red shine from the cooling forge and a few pale stars were all that illuminated his presence. The moon was in hiding behind black clouds. He came forward until he was close enough that Bran should have felt the warmth of his skin, but Bran felt only a chill, smelled copper, sharp and bittersweet between them.

"You don't believe me, but you should. Why would I lie to you—and if I'd never met you, how would I know you are Bran Fionnan?"

Bran shook his head again, but this time because he couldn't think of a way. He had spent painful months being told by his captors that he had no name, was worthy of none but what he was given—then they had called him Rud. Bran doubted the Milesians even remembered he had a name of his own any more, but *he* remembered. He had repeated it to himself when the world had seemed darkest to him, repeated it to prove that he hadn't always been unwanted. Everything else of the life he'd had before had faded into faint dreams, but not that

Bran looked up, nebulous feelings moving in him, but the stranger only laughed at him and Bran scowled and clenched his fists at his sides.

"Don't be so stubborn, Bran Fionnan."

"I'm not—"

The stranger took two steps more, and Bran felt the wall of the smithy against his back and silk against his skin again—and more than silk. There were hands on him, surprising, teasing, cool hands that stroked the warmth out of him. Bran thought about struggling, and the thought washed out of his mind before he could grasp it.

Why struggle? Why resist? What reason not to want this?

He was aware that the thoughts made no sense even as they took over his consciousness. He should resist, he should—a stranger, touching him like this…

The hands on him were as refreshing as the water had been, but they moved seeking intimate secrets. They stroked his chest, his nipples, his thighs, his buttocks, his back—Bran let out a groan and saw a smile full of sharp teeth drawing close to his throat. He had barely an instant for thoughts. He felt fear trying to come into being, a tightness in his stomach as the sharpness of those teeth and the coolness of the stranger's body, that copper odor, bound themselves up in one word. *Vampire.*

Despite the sudden knowledge, almost overwhelming, Bran felt the fear recede before it had come into being, superseded by reasonless trust. Without doubt, he knew suddenly that he was in no danger. He wouldn't be hurt, couldn't be hurt.

Not by this stranger.

Was it some kind of magic? Allure meant to make him accept his death? He had no reason to trust this stranger, but the more Bran tried to be afraid, the more he found he couldn't. There was only a vague panic that came from his inability to make sense out of his own emotions.

He felt an open-mouthed kiss against the vulnerable pulse below his jaw.

The stranger's tongue stroked Bran's throat and he felt desire and confusion warring in him. The sensations were exquisite, teeth scraping over his skin, following the path of that cool tongue. The bite Bran wanted to fear never came, just as he knew it wouldn't. There was only that teasing scrape of sharpness, immediately soothed by tongue. It was only a scratch, not even enough to draw blood, and as the shock began to release him, Bran felt his body responding to the presence of the *sidhe* bent over him. He heard a low murmur, questioning him, felt the hands on his skin retreat.

"Do you know me now, Bran Fionnan?"

Bran drew in a breath, expelled it.

"You are one of the *sidhe*. One of those vampires the Milesians are fighting."

Laughter defied Bran's words and he stared as the stranger finally pushed back his hood. Violet eyes gleamed brighter, almost indigo. His hair was long and red and braided with diamond beads, and a silver crown was on his head, a filigree of fangs and bones too elegant for their own grotesquery.

"I am not one of those vampires, I am *the* vampire."

Bran paled.

"Bran Fionnan, I am the Red King. I am Macsen Cadoc."

Bran felt a visceral lurch. Once again he expected terror and instead felt something different, something deeper. His eyes were fixed on Macsen's face, the cold, shadowed beauty of it. *Gods, I want him.* The thought flashed across Bran's consciousness like the lick of a whip, and he found himself fascinated by the curve of Macsen's lips, felt himself growing hard just looking. He wanted to be in that cool and tingling embrace again, wanted to feel the improbable chill that was the Red King's tongue against his throat. The Red King! What was wrong with him?

He knew by the gleam in Macsen's eyes that they were the same, that whatever strangeness, more than mortal, made Bran what he was, Macsen shared that thing. He knew it, just as he knew he wanted Macsen more than anyone he'd ever seen, but he didn't know why and that worried him.

Was it allure? A compulsion? There had to be something more than just this feeling, this feeling...like he had met Macsen before. Like he could *trust* him, even if that had to be the stupidest thing he had ever thought in his life. Trust the Red King!

Bran licked his lips and felt a pulse of sympathetic sensation in his groin. The irony — gods dark and sacred both, the irony! He knew the tug within himself for what it was, couldn't mistake the response of his body or the flicker in his thoughts. He had learned desire, had explored it with men and women in the village who had sought to seduce him and found themselves used instead.

"You're so quiet. You have no words?"

That voice again! It stroked Bran's skin like a pair of hands, teased him with its rich tones.

"What—what should I say?"

"You could say how much you want me, but I already know."

Bran felt a red flush blaze to life beneath his skin, but he didn't deny it.

"You're like me, that's why I want you, want to know you—to touch you—isn't it?"

Macsen only smiled at him, forced Bran to answer his own question.

"Just because I've never met another *sidhe* before, that has to be it—but I can't give in. I won't—"

"You won't?"

Macsen's fingers reached out and traced cool lines of sensation across Bran's skin.

"I won't."

The words burst from Bran, soft and hoarse.

"You're a killer, Macsen Cadoc."

Macsen stepped forward until Bran was flush against the wall, his palms flat against it, his fingers digging into the wood.

"I'm everything black in the night, Bran Fionnan. I'm death, and the shadows, and terror was everything to me until I caught the scent of you. I'm a killer, yes. That was why I came here, my first purpose...I am tired of these huntresses treating me as *prey*. But I won't hurt *you*. Not you. I couldn't if I tried."

Bran swallowed and blurted out the question looming in his thoughts before he could help himself.

"Why? And why do I *believe* you?"

Macsen smiled, expression unchanging, and leaned forward so that his mouth was just beside Bran's ear.

"You need a reason?"

Bran shivered beneath him and Macsen continued in a whisper that was only a breath above silence.

"*Why* is the bond between us."

"The bond — between us?"

"Do you really remember nothing? *Why* is the moon that is trusted to return after its night of darkness. *Why* is the wolf that howls in winter, loyal to his pack."

Bran stared into Macsen's face, saw something expectant there but shook his head. He didn't understand.

The bond between us, what is that?

"The wolf that — what? What's — ?"

Macsen's mouth moved down toward Bran's throat, and Bran felt those murmuring lips move against his skin.

"One day you'll know. Not today, Bran Fionnan. Not if you don't remember on your own."

Bran tried to protest, but between one breath and the next the presence of watchful malice that Macsen had sensed earlier intensified into something alert and vigilant. He held his hand pressed over Bran's mouth to silence him and felt some power reach out for his presence.

Now that Bran was here with him, in front of him, Macsen knew this feeling had nothing to do with him or the gold he forged. It was foreign power, not *sidhe* magic but something sour that pried at Macsen's flesh, Macsen's power...Macsen's secrets.

He lashed out at whatever was there with a wave of violent aura, and the closeness of the watchful presence retreated. Though it fell back, it didn't dissipate and Macsen scowled and came to a swift conclusion.

Milesians. Witch women!

But even if they knew Macsen was here, they couldn't have expected that he would come. The watchfulness was a part of this place, not aimed at him but at Bran.

They must watch him all the time. Every minute of every day — cowards! Spies! Ungrateful mortals!

Wrath rose up in Macsen like the awakening of a winter storm. His own suspicion infuriated him — was it the oath he had made, urging him onward? Perhaps. It didn't matter, the feeling was there and he would act on it. To do otherwise was not in his nature.

He bent his mouth to Bran's ear again and spoke low, but not in the whisper of before.

"We're being watched, Bran Fionnan."

At another time, for another reason, the shiver that moved over Bran's body then would have gratified Macsen greatly. Now, it only intensified his howling fury.

He is afraid.

At that moment, Macsen wanted nothing more than to turn and go down to the village and slay them all.

He focused on Bran instead, the rising gooseflesh, the shiver that hadn't quite subsided, the dryness of his lips, the hollow ache at the back of his gaze.

"You shouldn't worry, beautiful Bran."

Bran's answer came low and hoarse and angry. "No? You're not the one that has to deal with the consequences!"

"There are no consequences, Bran Fionnan. I'll take you away and you'll be mine."

Bran laughed, and Macsen stared. The sound surprised him.

"Take me away? No, I won't go with you. Not now, not ever—not unless I come to know you better. I won't lie and say I don't want you, but I'm not fool enough to run off and think myself safe with you, vampire. I want to live, and even *this* life is better than being nothing but a drink for you!"

Macsen smiled, but the expression was dark, his predator nature in full bloom. It had been a long time since he had been compelled to work for something or someone he wanted. He felt Bran shudder again, but the reason was different this time and Macsen knew it and enjoyed the trembling of Bran's skin beneath him.

"Vampire..."

Macsen drew out the word, tasted it and all its promises.

"You're wiser than you look, beautiful Bran. I, too, won't lie and say I don't want you, and I won't lie and say there is any such thing as being safe with me. But if you won't come, how do I keep you safe from *them*, Bran Fionnan?"

Bran stared at him, shook his head and let out a snort of disbelief. "You, keep me safe? Why would you—?" But Bran stopped and shook his head. "Never mind. It doesn't matter, I don't trust you."

"Yes, you do." Macsen thought Bran's scowl was as gorgeous as his smile. "Are you angry that I know you despite yourself? If you are angry, you should fight me."

"Fight you? I don't want to fight you, you're the first of my kind I've seen since...since a long time ago."

"But I'm not your kind, beautiful Bran. You are one of Summer's sons and I'm the Red King."

"You know what I mean, damn it! You're *sidhe*, just like I am!"

The line of Bran's jaw tightened and the blue of his eyes grew so dark it was indistinguishable from the night. Macsen was amused.

"You have your mother's eyes when you're angry, Bran Fionnan."

The rising flush of Bran's skin and the dark of his gaze both faded. He looked as if the wind had been knocked out of him, doubtful and desperate in a way that was painful to see.

"My — my mother? You know my real mother?"

"Of course I do. Didn't I say there was a bond between us? It was she who demanded it — to protect you from me. She is not very trusting, your mother."

Words tumbled out of Bran, a flood breaking a dam. "Tell me about her! What does she look like — do I really have her eyes — do I have siblings? Is my father with her, too? Have you met him? What is it like — the place I come from? Where — ?"

"You really do remember nothing. Bran Fionnan, I will answer all the questions you've asked me and any more you can think of — but only if you fight me. It's for your own good."

Macsen took a step back and gave him a sharp look, hoping Bran would understand his purpose.

"My own good? I've got no chance in a fight against you!"

The stroking of his ego pleased Macsen on one level, but he shook his head and pointed at the door that led to the forge.

"I'm willing to bet there's something in there that will help you — but you're forgetting that I won't hurt you. How could I make you mine if I hurt you?"

"You don't make any sense, Red King!"

"Don't I? There are consequences for every action and every inaction. Have you already forgotten what I told you? We are not alone here!"

Macsen heard Bran's sharp intake of breath, and knew that he had been understood. It wasn't a fight he wanted, it was the show of one. If the Milesians were watching, and he knew that they were, it would be better for Bran if he was seen to be resisting, fighting, even if there was no chance of his victory.

"It won't be so difficult—after all, you're the one that forges these weapons, aren't you? You should know how to use them."

He reached into his tunic and pulled out a knife with an edge that glinted gold.

Chapter Three

Bran burned to see what was in Macsen's hand, gleaming yellow, calling to him with his own power. It was the dagger Bran had made for Noirine. The dagger that had been meant to kill the Red King, this smug vampire standing in front of him with a smile on his face.

The old mix of fury and guilt rose up and choked him. The heart of his rage, close to the surface after a day spent brooding, had been soothed by the promise of Macsen's mouth and hands on his skin, had faded into the background confronted by something as inexplicable as this vampire presence and his own trust. Now instead of the pleasure those touches had promised, he was being goaded into a fight, and even knowing the reason didn't relieve the sting of Macsen's last comment.

'It won't be so difficult — after all, you're the one that forges these weapons, aren't you? You should know how to use them.'

Bran was aware that as of yet, the one he intended to fight had done nothing to him to warrant such a violent response. He was aware that it was unfair to take out twenty years' worth of pent up emotions on someone who had himself been hunted and harried for his existence alone.

The Milesians were fools, of course, to think they could influence or destroy the Red King and his court. Standing in Macsen's presence, he could see that now. He couldn't see what it was about Macsen that drove the Milesians to such extremes, seeking to destroy him, any more than he had ever been able to see what it was about himself that disgusted them so.

He was aware that men did not hold the wolf responsible for its kill, that the wildcat was not reviled for eating the flesh that sustained it. It was stupid to assume that men would have no predator, and completely idiotic to think that men could destroy such a predator if they found it.

It occurred to Bran that the Milesians had been badly misled by the ease with which their ancestors had banished the Irish *sidhe*, but that was a misconception that would only be corrected by future pain.

Bran looked up at Macsen, resolved to do what was necessary, and nodded once.

"All right. All right, I'll do what you want—and hold you to your promise, Red King."

Macsen smiled slowly. "*Sidhe* don't break their word like men, Bran. What I say, I will do. Now, choose a weapon!"

Blacker than the night sky, Macsen's aura flowed around Bran and buffeted him with power. Bran took a step to his left, his gaze fixed on Macsen, and reached behind him through the open door of the smithy. The staff was where he had left it, leaning against the wall just inside the threshold, and Bran grasped hold of it and squeezed it tightly. It hummed in his hands, drawing on the spark within him to further awaken the living gold in its bright, new spirals.

Bran faced his opponent and breathed deeply. He held the staff he had made poised across his body and saw Macsen stare at it, appraising. It was a gorgeous weapon, iron-hard oak capped and shod and inlaid with gleaming gold.

"Make a good show of it, Bran Fionnan!"

They rushed together and the lash of air that accompanied Macsen's movements was a blow on its own. Bran's thoughts overflowed in the wake of it. No wonder Noirine hadn't succeeded. How could she? She had been fast, but not fast enough, strong, but not as strong as the Red King.

Bran came back to himself to find that while he'd been distracted, Macsen had gained a steady grip on his staff. He stared at Macsen's hands, pale, smooth, the nails glinting like glass, then found himself flying over Macsen's shoulder and down onto the ground. Macsen tossed the weapon away from them into the night, and Bran sucked in a deep breath and met violet eyes with his own gaze. He saw promise in them, promise and lust and amusement.

That last irritated him, and he wondered if he might be able to make an impression. He had no weapon, but so what? The power inside him was what was dangerous, wasn't it?

Bran grinned and pushed himself onto his feet, crouched low to the ground and tracked Macsen's approach. When the Red King laid hands on him, exercised a tithe of his strength and lifted him, Bran dangled in his long-fingered grasp like a doll for half a moment. Then he reached for power and felt heat flood his flesh. His skin glowed with gold light, but

Macsen only laughed at him and squinted through the brightness.

"That won't do a thing, Bran Fionnan. Not *your* power, not to me. Not even you and the gold you wake together can harm me. It's just bad luck for you, none of your kin would have as much trouble. Weren't you listening? There's a bond between us, a bond neither of us can break. A bond of trust...and a bond against such dangers."

Bran understood nothing but that he had failed, but he wasn't too unhappy, just confused. He hadn't really wanted to hurt Macsen, after all.

Macsen put him down, but his hands held Bran still, and Bran twisted in struggle. He didn't know if he was struggling for show, or because of his own internal conflicts, and he didn't know if what came next was an accident or not. Was it because he pressed too hard, moved just too far trying to get away? Was it just because Macsen wanted it, even as Bran himself did?

A kiss.

Bran closed his eyes and welcomed the tongue that slipped past his lips. He went still in Macsen's grasp. All the nerves in his body flared in one moment and questioned Bran's inner silence for the truth, but he had no answers. Bran savored the taste of the Red King and his forbidden kiss while it lasted, responded with the press of his body and the willingness of his mouth. He felt Macsen pull away from him and held back a moan of discontent. It was wrong, it had to be wrong, but it felt *right*.

Bran panted and looked up at Macsen as he stepped back with a gaze made rich by lust.

"Beautiful, Bran—but I want you all to myself when I convince you to come with me. Wait for me. Tomorrow night, I will return."

Bran's eyes darted anxiously from one dark corner to the next, as if he could see the one watching them.

"They'll still be watching, they're *always* watching."

"It doesn't matter if they're watching if they can't see, Bran Fionnan."

Then he was gone.

* * * *

Bran stood stunned in the darkness. Maybe he had melted, maybe he had gone up in fire—or was it both? Bran sucked in deep breaths of night air and felt his heart pound frantic and greedy inside his chest. His lips burned, and his skin tingled with the memory of Macsen's hands and their coolness.

It was only then that Bran realized that he was still naked. He had left his tunic and apron and trousers by the barrel and never stopped to put them on. He wondered what an outsider would think—one nude goldsmith, confronting the Red King! Bran shook his head, and went to his clothes, still on the ground where he had left them. The barrel was still there, only half full now, and Bran looked down into it as he passed by and saw the moon reflected there.

The sky had cleared, but Bran's thoughts didn't mimic what he saw reflected on the water. What did it mean, this visit of the Red King? A *sidhe*—not one of his own kind but a *sidhe* none the less. A dangerous being, an inhuman creature...beautiful though. Beautiful, and so tempting...

"You're a fool, Bran Fionnan. You should've taken the chance while you had it, just to get out of here..."

Now that he was alone, he could begin to admit how much he wanted to get away. He went down the hill and found the staff Macsen had tossed away by its gleam in the moonlight. He went in through the door to the smithy and put the staff by his table — it would need polishing tomorrow, someone would be coming for it soon. He banked the fire and made sure he hadn't left anything dangerous lying around, then went through into the main house and tossed his clothes to one side and himself to the other.

He lay on his furs beside the fire, staring into the shifting shades of red, thinking of his visitor, his promises, the danger and what might be the truth...

His sleep was deep and shadowed.

Heavy dreams filled him, in which Macsen's hands were on him and did not stop. He woke to white spilled in his furs as if he were an untried boy. A few more hours of sleep gave him dreams of Macsen in motion, running, flying. He felt the enjoyment Macsen felt as he moved over the water of the Irish Sea, and Bran woke again, startled, because it was far too real. The tang of seasalted air was still in his nose, and Macsen's presence was strong around him.

Alone in the first hour of the dawn, alone with his thoughts and his memory, Bran tried to make himself forget the fascinating presence of the Red King. He tried to convince himself that his desire was wrong, but it was hard. *Impossible.* He had lived too long without the little touches, words and fingertips that make up and enrich a life. Bran couldn't deny the irresistible pull he felt toward those cool hands, those violet eyes. Even now, he found himself wanting, thinking, focused. He muttered to himself while he prodded the fire into life.

"I should go to the huntresses, but I won't. I can't. The only *sidhe* I've ever met—how could I? It's not like they don't know already. And he said he'd be back tonight—"

A little at a time, Bran fed kindling to the flames then tossed on larger logs.

"And who was watching? *Somebody*. Gods, why does it have to be him that I want?"

Bran moaned his trouble to no one. Inside and out, except for him the morning was still and soundless. People would be waking in the village soon, but he was too far from it for casual sounds to intrude.

Now that Noirine was dead, his only contact would be with those who came to order and collect their commissions. If he disobeyed...but he did not disobey. Not anymore. The first and only time he had ever gone against an order had taught him a lesson in pain he had not challenged since, as well as a lesson in what he was to expect from his new kin. No warmth. No love. Just enough to sustain him, never anything more.

The memory of his minutes with Macsen was more than any of that. Bran faced the feeling openly, but he couldn't give it a name. What should he call so much desire? What should he call the *other* thing—the impossible trust, the fading of all fear...what should he call that? Where did it come from? Macsen's words flashed into his thoughts.

There is a bond between us.

Bran said it out loud, questioning, confused. "There is...a bond between us."

He licked his lips as if Macsen's kiss might still linger. He tried to turn his thoughts away from the hope that kept forming inside him, the questions it shaped itself into.

What did the Red King know about his mother? About his family, his *real* family?

Would he really be safe if he left here and went away with the Red King?

Would the Red King really return tonight?

"Macsen Cadoc..." The name slipped from his tongue far too easily.

"You owe me answers."

Bran turned away from the fire to look at the door.

"You had *better* come back."

* * * *

Macsen sped away from Bran Fionnan with his thoughts roaring in his head. He had only wanted to rid himself of an irritation — to go back to the days before his court had been interrupted by the danger of someone hunting them. He had planned simply and swiftly. It wasn't to be war, there would be no warnings or promises, no prisoners or symbolic victories. He would make an end of the Milesians as a threat to his kind, even if he couldn't kill them all. He would do to them everything they sought to do to him and his.

"But you, Bran Fionnan..."

Macsen tasted the name and was pleased by it, even as he was confused by his own actions. He had sipped at Bran's breath and not at his blood, hadn't sought even a drop, despite the temptation. Why not? True, it was not good manners to drink from other *sidhe* without permission, but...

But.

He didn't understand how a single person could be the source of so many conflicting thoughts.

The thought of Bran's blood exalted the thirst within him, made it scream with want and need, but he hadn't yet tried it and still he knew that blood alone wouldn't be enough. Was that knowledge enough to explain why he had delayed his vengeance? He had achieved half his purpose, that much was true. He had found the one who forged those dangerous weapons, even if he hadn't managed any destruction.

Macsen was prepared to risk much for another kiss like that first, so sweet.

Several things were already clear to him, even from that single, short encounter. Bran barely understood his own nature, was more human than fae. He had been raised away from his own kind, and he didn't know there was a bond between him and Macsen. He didn't remember that a fragile peace hung on his shoulders, had no conception of how his mother still mourned his loss.

"And he wants me…"

Macsen closed his eyes and envisioned Bran as he had just seen him, the water pooling in his navel, beading on his skin, gooseflesh rising in the wake of the evening's breeze.

The image called up all his perceptions of that moment, furnace odors, heat, the tingle of gold in the air and on Bran's skin, growing as Bran turned to confront him. There had been desire in Bran's eyes, and in the awakening of his body—desire bound up with fury, an enticing, enthralling combination. Smooth limbs, lean, strong muscles, naked skin everywhere Macsen's hands had touched or tried to grasp, naked skin slick with dampness. *That kiss.*

"That kiss—I couldn't resist. I shouldn't have done it, but I couldn't resist."

Macsen tapped his fingers against his lips, remembering. All he had now was salt spray, but the memory was strong enough to make even the sea taste sweet.

"I want Bran Fionnan. I want more than his blood, I want his whole being—I want all of him to belong only to me!"

The night had no answer for his declaration.

Macsen had had lovers across the centuries, pets and playthings, men and women, *sidhe* and stranger for the endless hours of night in his kingdom beneath the hill. This...this want, this desire was something different. This was a new feeling, or why should one kiss matter when it never had before? The oath he had sworn, the bond that the oath had forged between him and Bran Fionnan—was that the reason? To trust...to be loyal. Never to harm and to help if he could.

No. Not the oath.

Why would such an oath make him burn? It would not.

No.

Sea wind whipped across his face, and Macsen breathed deeply of the chill, damp air. Mere want wasn't enough to explain his feeling. Was there something else that might explain the intensity of his desire, the rush that had overcome him the moment he had first laid eyes on Bran?

"It wasn't even the sight of you, it was that scent, lightning crushed against the sun. Bran Fionnan...if it isn't enough to want you—do I need you, too?"

He spoke to test the thought.

"I *need* you. But—why?"

The Red King clenched his fists, came to the shore of his own island and turned his gaze in the direction he had come from. He wanted nothing so much as to go back right now, this instant—but he would be patient. He would let Bran spend a day wondering whether or not he would come back. He wanted Bran to catch himself hoping for Macsen's return, wanted Bran to step toward him when he returned, and not away.

"Tonight, I'll come for you and I'll find out."

The Red King laughed a little as he passed over the threshold of the barrow that led into his own kingdom. For the first time in a thousand years, he was not bored. His nerves tingled with excitement and the promise of his feeling.

"Tonight, Bran Fionnan."

The words fell from his lips and followed him away from the rising sun.

* * * *

Bran spent the day learning how to wait. He was tense, jumped at small sounds and found himself at the door often, looking out at nothing—waiting, always waiting. By mid-morning, he was despairing and sure that Macsen would never return. By noon, he had changed his mind and decided that Macsen would definitely come. Why would he have said so otherwise? To taunt him?

Macsen would come back. Macsen would come back, or Macsen wouldn't have kissed him.

The words became his mantra, the only reassurance he had.

The day was full of tension, of promise. Bran spent a few hours polishing mud and grass stains off the staff he had finished the night before, and caught himself in fantasies that spurned all his attempts to turn them away. Whether or not Macsen was deserving of trust,

Bran felt it. Whether or not there was a point to desiring him, Bran *did*.

When he was finished with the staff he cooked food that he didn't eat, put it away again and paced restlessly.

He found himself at the threshold again before he knew it. He stared at the western sky, crimson now, and felt the sunset light paint his features with heat. With closed eyes, he stood there until the warmth was gone and the dull orange glow had faded from behind his eyelids. He looked up at the sky and saw the pink edge of twilight darkening to rich purple.

A tingle crossed his skin.

It'll be night soon. He's coming – the Red King is coming!

His eyes snapped away from the horizon at the pressure of some inner call. The presence that he had felt the night before, a great, dark cloaking of power, was near him. He could feel it, and as he did so he felt the awakening of his own strange nature, the *sidhe* essence with which he had almost no experience. He had only ever touched the power within him to forge the weapons that were required of him. Anything else would have been seen as dangerous.

There were many among the huntresses, witches and warriors both, who wanted him dead. It sullied them to be helped by him — that they thought this and he knew it was one of the only comforts he had. At the moment, however, thinking about the number of Milesian women who wanted him dead was no comfort.

Yesterday, someone had been watching, one of those witch-women most likely. They would pay twice as much attention tonight. Macsen's visit could cause trouble, but what had he said?

"Watching doesn't matter...if you can't see. Does that mean he can hide us? Prevent them? That could be dangerous, too."

Bran had a feeling of foreboding then, in the bruised moments before the twilight faded into the dark. Then it was too late, and the sky was black and starstruck, and in the next moment an aura of overwhelming shadow brushed across Bran's skin like a physical touch.

He looked up, and the Red King appeared at the crest of the hill, moving toward him with quick, even steps. He stopped a few paces away and Bran smiled despite himself, but made no move to go closer. Macsen didn't hesitate. He crossed the narrow space between them and reached out to touch Bran's face, passed his thumb over Bran's cheek, drew deadly, delicate fingers against Bran's lips. Bran stood utterly still and felt his nerves come alive with fire and the knowledge that he wanted this man—this male—he wanted him, danger be damned, and he would have him.

He would *live*, just this once, even if later it killed him. Desire surged over him, undeniable.

"You—"

Macsen leaned forward and drew Bran toward him in the same instant, enclosed Bran's body in his embrace, bent to him and gave him the kiss that Bran had been missing through the empty hours of the day. Macsen's mouth was sweet, his lips soft, all promise, but Bran succumbed for only an instant then pulled back.

"You came—"

"Of course I came, didn't I say I would? I'm not in the habit of saying things I don't mean."

"You shouldn't have come. The Milesians—"

"Will see nothing. I brought shadow with me, didn't you feel it? Don't you feel it now? If I had been prepared last night I wouldn't have asked you to fight me, but you are safe now."

Bran drew in a deep breath, then nodded. "I did, I *do*, but—"

"No worries, Bran Fionnan. If one of those women turns her power in this direction, she will see only the night. It's not a person that watches you, but a witch's power. I felt it when I first arrived yesterday, but I thought it was trained on me—yet I thought on it and that's not so, is it?"

Bran stared a little then looked away, scowling.

"It's to watch me, but I don't even know why they bother."

Macsen smiled and Bran stared, his attention caught on the sharp points of Macsen's teeth.

"You don't know, Bran?"

"Like you do—"

"They *fear* you. They fear your nature, your essence, your being. That you exist terrifies them, just as it terrified them to discover me—surely you know this? They're fanatics, it's obvious. I saw it in that girl, your sister...what was her name?"

Bran frowned in irritation.

"Her name was Noirine, but she was *not* my sister. And that reminds me—you promised me answers, yesterday. About my mother, and my family. I haven't forgotten, Macsen Cadoc!"

Macsen smiled at him. "And you remember my name. I had started to wonder, yesterday. When you kept calling me *Red King*."

Bran flushed, and Macsen reached out and drew him close again, nuzzled his cheek and kissed his jaw, the curve of his ear, then down again toward his mouth. This kiss was rougher, deeper, and Bran tasted blood without knowing whose lip he had bitten. One of Macsen's hands ran through his hair, dragged sharp nails against his scalp, held his head still. Despite himself, Bran groaned and gave in to his own desire. The soft lips opened to Bran's tongue. He felt cool, tingling hands reach up to touch his cheeks, felt them running through his hair, slip down around his shoulders.

Bran turned his head under the pressure of a nudge and another kiss, and Macsen pulled him into a closer embrace. Bran opened his eyes and the movement felt lazy. Was the Red King's kiss a drug?

No. It's just desire.

Bran licked his lips, a quick darting of his tongue. He felt Macsen's eyes on the motion and knew then the inevitable end of this confrontation.

"You're trying to distract me, but I want—"

"I don't want to talk about your mother right now, Bran Fionnan. I don't want to talk at all. Not now. Ask me anything you want, but later. *Not now.*"

He leaned close, breathed deeply. Bran felt Macsen's breath against his lips and tried once more, but he was pressing up against Macsen even as he spoke, even as his words became a murmur that washed against Macsen's lips.

"You're sure no one—?"

"No one will see us tonight. Not unless it's someone with more power than *me.*" Macsen's voice was breathless, his eyes shining and dark, the pupils dilated with lust. "Now, don't struggle. I'd never hurt you, beautiful Bran—"

Macsen licked Bran's lips, so soft, so teasing. Bran knew what was about to happen the moment before it did, but in that moment he found that he didn't care.

He had accepted Macsen's nature for what it was—he enjoyed it, darkness and all. It was proof that Macsen was like him, proof that he was *sidhe*. Bran's want flowed hot in him, spurring him onward, and beside his lust was the same welling of inexplicable trust that he had felt the night before. *Trust*. It was a promise with no words that was reinforced by Macsen's aura, Macsen's presence.

Macsen smirked, his lips stretching over white teeth, then bent to Bran's throat. Bran felt Macsen's tongue against his skin. Sharp teeth penetrated deep. A tickle like the brush of a feather became twin needles of sensation and fluttering heat. Bran gasped. The feeling was nothing like what he had imagined.

The theft of his blood was a delicate seduction that gave him promises instead of pain. For a moment it let him feel the rich, dark core of Macsen's being—but that moment was very short. Macsen had taken barely a mouthful from Bran's veins, but he was already stepping back.

"Delicious."

Macsen's hands roamed Bran's skin through untied, unlaced clothes. Dazed, Bran wondered when that had happened. Macsen's touch aroused, stimulated, tempted. His fingers teased Bran's nipples into hard points and his other hand slipped between the tight press of their bodies and grasped the straining stiffness of Bran's erection. Macsen lifted his lips from Bran's throat and soothed the shallow wound there with his tongue. For a moment a haze hung across Macsen's eyes. Bran saw it, heard Macsen's voice thicken and slow and soften into a murmur that brushed heat against the tender place on his throat.

"Be my lover, beautiful Bran, my lover..."

Bran didn't know why Macsen had stopped to ask. It felt like he had wanted this touch, this moment, forever. It didn't matter that need and desire weren't really the same thing, not right now. He surprised himself with the force of his answer. "*Yes.*"

That one word seemed like it was enough to awaken the bestial promise that slept in the Red King. Bran felt the shift in the hands that pulled his clothes from his body, hands that grasped his throbbing erection and pulled pleasure from his loins with smooth, slow strokes.

They stumbled together, and came up against the wall of Bran's house. Macsen held Bran pinned there with the weight of his body, and Bran slipped his fingers against Macsen's chest and down, down — he needed no encouragement to return the pleasure that Macsen's stroking fingers gave him.

He could feel Macsen's pulse beating in the heavy hardness that slid back and forth across his palm — then their gasps were equal and they panted together, gasping, moaning. Bran's head fell forward against Macsen's chest. He heard his own voice calling out, strangled and broken.

"Macsen...Macsen...Macsen..."

Macsen was quieter, but his whisper, "Bran," was tender and sharp enough to send a new shudder rolling over Bran's skin.

Macsen recovered first, and lifted his forehead from Bran's shoulder. He pulled Bran away from the wall and woke him from the haze of his climax with a kiss, with many kisses, with touches. Bran stepped back over the threshold, pushed the door open behind him, and Macsen pushed him across the bare floor to the furs that lay beside the hearth.

They tumbled together onto them, and Bran gasped at the sensation of fur against the new sensitivity of his skin, then again at the renewed tugging of Macsen's fingers around his erection. Bran was as hard as if nothing had happened between them, but he had no leisure to contemplate this. Macsen's tongue swept across the planes of his chest and laved his nipples. Slender fingers caressed the heavy sac drawn up close to Bran's arousal, then dipped downward.

"Mac — ah!"

The cry tore past his lips as Macsen slipped a finger inside him. He thrust his hips back against Macsen's hand and Macsen's tongue flickered out over his lips. A hot flush moved down from Bran's cheeks to his throat, spread across his chest, dipped into every hollow of his abdomen. A second finger joined the first, and for a moment Bran squirmed in discomfort, but the pleasure was greater.

Macsen seemed intent on drawing him into an ecstatic web from which he would never escape. Bran's erection wept clear fluid, and his mouth opened in a dark O of pleasure. Macsen made two fingers three, and Bran thrust his hips into each stroke of Macsen's hand.

When Macsen pulled his fingers away, Bran lay panting for a moment, then sat up and silenced himself with the taste of Macsen's body, with the hard, heated length of his erection. Macsen let out a hiss of pleasant shock and stared down into Bran's eyes. He clenched his fists in Bran's hair, and Bran gloried in the tugging of Macsen's fingers.

Bran stroked the underside of Macsen's cock with his tongue, teased the most sensitive spots. The coolness of Bran's indrawn breath moved over Macsen's rigid shaft, and Bran laved his tongue over the softer head then down again to tease beneath, over and over and over.

Macsen groaned, and leaned down and pushed Bran away, lifted him just enough to kiss him then held him back against the furs. Bran spread his legs wide and reached out his arms for Macsen's hips.

"You are mine now, beautiful Bran—"

There was a shock for Bran when Macsen entered him, but it wasn't painful. Macsen thrust slowly, to give Bran time to adjust, and Bran tightened his body around Macsen's intrusion and coaxed his nerves.

"*Ahh...*Bran—"

Muscles clenched in Bran's buttocks. His fingers reached out and grasped hold of Macsen's thighs. He licked his lips, begged until Macsen's slow thrusts quickened, roughened with every cry that made its way past Bran's lips. Bran had never imagined this sensation was possible. Pleasure sparked in wild stardust patterns inside his body, shot from the head of Macsen's cock inside him to the hard length of his own erection. He felt it pressed tight between them, massaged by the movement of Macsen's body against him.

Sensation flooded his nerves.

Bran let his hands rift across Macsen's nipples, pinched them lightly and pulled them with shaking fingers. Macsen growled at that, reared back and pounded into Bran. He slid his hands from Bran's thighs to his ankles, lifted his legs and spread them wider. The indigo grew dark in his eyes. Every thrust brought a splash of unimaginable pleasure.

Bran wrapped his legs around Macsen's hips and closed his eyes tightly, held on to the furs beneath him, to the ground, to Macsen—Macsen—

So good. Bran shuddered and arched as the white fire of his climax ripped through him. Vaguely, from a sated, delirious distance, he heard his voice rise, a loud, groaning cry. He felt the pulsing release of wetness against his belly and deep inside him as they spilled their pleasure together.

Mixed with his own moans were Macsen's—a perfect sound. Macsen leaned forward and his mouth covered Bran's, a deeper kiss than all the others put together. His lips strayed down to Bran's throat, and Bran reached up and embraced his new lover even as he felt Macsen's teeth penetrate the wound at his throat and make it deeper.

Bran felt no fear, only another dark, sweet rush.

* * * *

Bran Fionnan. Starlight and moonlight and one thousand years beneath the sun.

Macsen's eyelids fluttered closed and he knew only taste as his teeth went deep into Bran's flesh and brought him a flavor straight from the core of Bran's being. He had taken only a drop earlier, only enough to wet his tongue. Now he filled himself from the beating of Bran's heart, a heart that was gold all the way through. Bran's power came flowing into his mouth with the blood, a sleeping danger that beat yet did not burn as Macsen drank it down.

Such blood from another of Summer's people would be like deadly fire, but in Bran he tasted the flames without being burned by them. —

Macsen's thoughts scattered in the presence of so much richness. Bran's blood was the essence of the sun, distilled away from all darkness yet stripped of its danger. Again and again Macsen swallowed ichor as clean and pure as light. It was dim and distantly that Macsen finally felt Bran begin to fade in his embrace, heard Bran's heartbeat straining in his grasp with all the fluttering speed and vulnerability of a hummingbird.

He let go, licked his lips and smiled, staggered back and realized belatedly that such blood, more than human, brighter than any blood he had ever tasted before, was as heavy in him as a thousand cups of wine. He shook his head, and spoke, but his words came out slurred and unfocused. The gray shadows of the room around him wavered before his eyes.

"Mine, all mine, Bran Fionnan. Mine forever—forever, all...all mine..."

Macsen passed into unconsciousness with his last word leaning on his lips.

* * * *

Bran stared down at the unconscious shape of the Red King with one hand clamped to the wound at his throat. It wasn't dangerously deep, but it was still bleeding and now that Macsen was off him it burned with the pain he hadn't felt while he was being bitten. Bran rolled over and stood unsteadily, then reached out with one foot to prod the still shape. Macsen didn't stir and Bran laughed, but only a little.

"So this is what happens when the Red King comes for you. The terror of the eastern island...Macsen Cadoc."

The name flowed off Bran's tongue, and he swayed, dizzy from blood loss but unwilling to fall beside his lover. What had he been thinking? The night before he had laughed and said he wouldn't give in, but here he was, and he had done much, much more than just give in. If Bran was honest with himself, and he had no reason not to be, he didn't want to take back anything that had happened, he just wanted more. More touch, more pleasure, more darkness—more of Macsen Cadoc.

Bran stood over Macsen and stared down at him. The face before him had a similarity to Bran's own face—angles, curves, planes, shadows. His own eyes were cobalt, not lavender-indigo, but the same unnatural gleam resided in both their gazes...or at least it did when Macsen was awake.

"Why do I trust you, Macsen Cadoc? Your strength doesn't frighten me...your bloodlust doesn't frighten me even when it should. I don't understand."

Bran contemplated his questions while he stared down at Macsen, but he came up with no answers. The Red King lay in the furs of his bed, lay with Bran's own scent on his skin. There was danger in it, and a thrill that went along with that danger. Part of him *wanted* to be caught with Macsen. He wanted the Milesians to know that he'd betrayed them in the worst way possible, that he'd chosen their most terrible enemy over them.

Part of him was terrified of what would happen if they found out the truth, but more than either of those feelings, he was caught up in a personal revelation that was too important to cast aside for caution's sake. To Bran's certain knowledge, Macsen Cadoc was the only other being like himself that he had met since the Milesians had stolen him. Macsen said that they weren't the same, that he was winter's shadow and Bran was summer's light—but that didn't matter to Bran. Macsen and his kind shared Bran's *sidhe* nature, and nothing else was important.

Bran's eyes remained fixed on Macsen while all these things raced through his head. It hadn't escaped him that their positions had reversed, that it was Bran who had the advantage now, who held the upper hand despite the fact that his strength was almost nothing compared to the one who lay unconscious on the ground before him.

Bran crouched by the fire and stirred the embers into life, his mind mimicking the flickering flame. For long minutes he stayed there, then turned to look at the still, smiling figure on his furs. Bran's eyes lingered on Macsen's face, on the glow of his hair in the firelight, brighter red, and on the smooth lines of his features.

"You could be mine, Macsen Cadoc. If you meant what you said — if it wasn't blood-drunk rambling — "

He surprised himself, saying the words aloud, but it didn't matter. There was no one to hear but himself, after all. That was...almost disappointing. He shook his head. What was he thinking? Still...

"If you want me to be yours then you'll have to be mine, Macsen Cadoc."

Bran lay with his back to the fire and his thoughts stayed restless, but he couldn't come to a resolution. It was too soon, the emotions too fresh and his nerves speaking too loudly.

"Macsen...Cadoc..."

He fell asleep with the name on his lips.

Chapter Four

Macsen woke painfully to the yellow rays of the sun shining through the window on the eastern wall. Brightness pierced Macsen's eyelids, and he pushed himself back out of the reach of the sun and immediately felt better. He scowled across the room at the light, rubbing his eyes, but his expression softened when his gaze fell on Bran, still asleep on the other side of the hearth.

Bran was curled around himself, his head pillowed on one arm, his legs drawn up toward his chest. The other arm was flung out toward the fire, curled fingers resting on the lip of the hearth. He turned just a little and stretched and Macsen smirked to himself as the dark bruise on Bran's throat became visible.

"Such blood, such blood!" He spoke in the barest whisper and licked his lips as if he could taste it again. "I'll be better prepared next time. I'll sip at you like strong wine, Bran Fionnan."

There *would* be a next time. Macsen had already made up his mind. Despite the weight of centuries on his shoulders and the promise of eternity to come, he was an impatient being. He needed Bran to be his, to be with him always, to be beside him in his bed and in his life. He needed Bran to sit with him over the Red Court, to move beside him in the endless flowing of the dance. Macsen had never been denied before, and he wasn't going to start now. Not with Bran.

Macsen moved smoothly around the hearth, then lay behind his lover and felt Bran shudder against him, flinch away then press back against his chest. The heat of Bran's blood had long dissipated and he knew Bran felt a chill from his presence, but the warmth of Bran's body was enough for both of them.

Macsen was drawn to that heat as a moth is drawn to flame. He leaned on one elbow and reached with the other hand to brush stray hairs away from Bran's face. His fingers stroked Bran's hip, the top of his thigh, and he looped his arm around Bran's waist and breathed heat from the curve of his shoulder. In his sleep, Bran murmured Macsen's name and smiled. Macsen felt a glow within himself that was almost physical and purely startling.

"There are many who miss you, Bran Fionnan, but I think I want to keep you to myself for just a little longer. I — don't want to share you."

Macsen pressed his lips to Bran's shoulder then stood, his mind made up. His thoughts grew clear as he gathered up his clothes and dressed. He would take Bran away with him, bring him into his own kingdom. He would keep Bran for himself. He turned then, intending to reach down and take Bran into his arms, but his actions were restrained.

In the instant of his intent he was stilled, couldn't move a muscle.

A pulse of darkness bound Macsen. He felt it as a physical thing, so tight that if it had been anything but magic it would have cut bone deep in the first moment. He could see what it was that restrained him, shackles of shadow gray and black and gleaming. Macsen pulled against them but couldn't move. The restraining power was strong enough to hold him no matter how he struggled, strong enough that even his prodigious strength wasn't enough to break them.

His eyes widened when he realized what it was that had hold of him, and he scowled as he forced himself to relax, to put aside all thoughts of taking Bran away with him. As he did so the restraining power faded, and he knew that he had guessed correctly.

The shackles had been forged by the bond between him and Bran. They responded to the terms of the oath he had sworn. It wasn't only that he couldn't do harm to Bran, he was also prevented from betraying Bran's trust. The trust Bran had put in him the night before when he had said 'no, I won't go with you', and had fallen asleep believing the words were enough.

Macsen was frustrated. This meant convincing had to be done, meant that Bran had to say *yes* to him, couldn't be coerced or stolen. To take, that was Macsen's nature...but to claim Bran for his own he would have to convince instead.

He bent over Bran again. This time he intended to wake him, to tempt him with promises and truths, with the answers that he had asked for and some that he hadn't. His hand was in motion, his fingertips close to Bran's shoulder when he heard a shout and jerked back.

The sound of many feet coming up the hard dirt road that led down to the village was clear to him when he turned his attention outside, and Macsen heard the sounds of voices speaking, many more than just the one that had let out the shout that had alerted him.

In one moment decision confronted him. Stay or go? Fight or flee? It was daylight and his opponents would be numerous. There was no danger to Macsen, not even if he had to brave the dawn to fight his way free, but there was danger to Bran. That made up his mind.

"It seems you must wait a little longer, Bran Fionnan — and so must I."

In a flicker of movement and shadow, he passed out the door and down the hillside on the other side of the house, away from the approaching voices. Bran would wonder where he had gone, he knew. With luck, Bran would miss him and would be waiting for him when he came back. Then it would be easy to make him change his mind, to get him to agree to leave this world behind.

Swiftly, Macsen passed over the green land and made his way home across the sea.

* * * *

Bran awoke to the sound of a loud and rapid knock on his door. He jerked upright and looked around, confused and disoriented. He was on the other side of the fire from where he usually slept, and the angle of the sunlight that came through the window told him that it was late, several hours past dawn. The sound of the knock that had woken him lingered on the air.

He looked around for Macsen, but it was apparent in half a moment that he was alone. The Red King had vanished, had left neither the imprint of his body nor so much as a single strand of hair behind. Bran felt a bit of pain that there had been no goodbye, no further promise.

"But what was I expecting? It's not like—it's not like there was a reason for him to stay—"

Bran cut himself off as the knock was repeated. He heard voices outside and stood with a jerk. He recognized one voice in particular, and didn't like to hear it.

"Dealla—of course. It had to be Dealla."

His heart sank. Princess, huntress, witch, she was one of his least favorite people in the world. If Dealla was here, it was to pick up the staff he had just finished and to leave a new commission. With Macsen gone there was no reason to worry now, but he had hoped...*what? What had I hoped? For something to change?* Bran sighed and pushed himself to his feet just as he heard a heavy hand knock on the door for a third time.

He cast around until he found his trousers, then tied them on and took the staff in his hand from where it sat on the table. He went to the door then and opened it, wiping the sleep away from his eyes with one hand. The little girl who stood in front of him was obviously not the one who had knocked, and Bran was surprised into silence—he had been preparing cool remarks for Dealla.

His gaze slid away from the child and up to the woman he had expected. Dark red hair drawn back beneath a gold circlet, gold at her throat and on her arms and wrists, Dealla looked every inch the princess that she was, but she was standing well away from the door, not even glancing in Bran's direction.

He turned his attention back to the girl and contemplated her youth and poise. Her face was very serious, her eyes wide and green and dark. Freckles splashed her cheeks but not her nose, and her red hair was held back by a polished band of silver that bore an amber stone. She was a solemn, pretty little thing, and though he knew what she must have come for Bran crouched down to her level and peered at her face.

"Well, are you going to introduce yourself, girl? You have a heavy knock for a little one."

"It wathn't me. The warrior did it."

She pointed at a tall, armored member of the king's guard, and Bran was amused. So many, just as entourage for one little girl and a princess with a request? The king was getting paranoid in his old age.

"Well, girl, you must be very important if the king's guard knocks for you. I'm Bran Fionnan. What's your name and house?"

He saw Dealla's lips tighten out of the corner of his eye and almost took back his words. How many years had it been since he'd dared to use his name among them? But the girl in front of him didn't know any better, and spine straight, lisping, she recited the answers he'd asked for.

"I'm Saoirse Saorla, of the house of the King! I'm the...the third princess, and um...oh! And I've come to collect my staff, sir, please."

Bran held back his laughter, but he couldn't hold back a grin, nor a bit of a wince that smoothed away quickly. Saoirse Saorla! An unfortunate name for a lisping child. "A princess! And no one told me. My house isn't fit for such a princess, it's a good thing I brought this outside with me. For you, My Lady."

Bran went down on one knee and held out the staff he had brought with him. Saoirse's eyes went wide and she reached out her fingertips and touched it gently.

"It's so pretty! It's really — it's really for me?"

"Of course. A beautiful lady needs a beautiful weapon."

Bran let it roll out of his hands and into the girl's. She was too short by far to wield it properly, but the receiving of such arms was a rite of passage for a huntress now. He had rarely met one so young, but then he had known it was for a child, after all. It surprised him more that it was for the king's own daughter — didn't he care for her life? Despite the fact that the girl was Milesian, Bran felt compassion for her. She was so little — she was being used as much as he was, poor thing.

"Saoirse Saorla, daughter of the King, this staff is yours. *Yours.* It will protect you, if you can learn to handle it with skill. This is a weapon of power, and that means it's more than a killing tool. Grow, and it will grow with you. That is something I've learned, My Lady. Remember, I made it special, just for you."

Bran stood then, and turned to look at Dealla, still standing silent with a disinterested expression on her narrow face.

"Well, *Princess*? Is that all you've come for, or do you have more work for me to do?"

Dealla looked at her fingernails, and rested her other hand on the knife she carried at her waist.

"Work, traitor?"

Bran's posture stiffened. He had been called that before, but not by her. Her father had said it, the only time Bran had tried to disobey. Why would she say it now? His thoughts flashed to Macsen's face and he knew with the dark instinct that works to provide terrible truths that Dealla was aware he'd had a visitor the night before.

Bran tried to smooth his thoughts, to erase the presence of Macsen from his mind, to wipe all fear, all darkness from his soul, but that was impossible.

How does she know? Didn't he say no one would see? Didn't he say — but it doesn't matter. She knows — she knows he was here — it's on her face —

Dealla came close to him, very close, and moved her sister out of the way with a gesture and a reassuring smile.

"Well done, Saoirse, but remember — he's not a man, he's a beast. A dangerous creature, don't forget it, hmm?"

Bran watched the girl's scrutiny move between him and her sister. Hesitantly, she nodded, and Bran saw her begin to gasp before his vision was blocked by a fist made heavy by the weight of a knife. The blow dazed him, and as he blinked and reached up to press his hand to his temple he felt a prick of steel at his throat, a pulse of familiar power. He looked down past the short, gleaming blade of Dealla's gilded knife, a knife he had forged himself, and focused on her face.

"The punch was not your punishment, traitor. Punishment will come later. *That* was for speaking to my sister in such a way. Did you think I hadn't noticed? The way you thought no one had noticed your little tryst last night...or the night before? Perhaps your vampire lover has strength enough to blind the powers that watched you, but being blinded is enough for me to know that something was happening that you wanted to hide."

"You —"

Dealla smiled, a cruel expression that lifted her upper lip over her teeth.

"*Me*. Yes, I know all about it. Did you think you were ever free, that you were ever not being watched?

I always have my sight on you, power stalking you, tracking your every movement."

Bran tightened his fists and swallowed past the knife pressed against his throat. He knew now why she had brought a dozen of the King's Guard with her. If she had come with only one or two, nothing would have restrained him. Dealla stared into his face and laughed.

"You really didn't know? What a fool! As if we would ever leave a creature like you free to roam where he wanted among men! My father thought there would be no reason to keep track of you after your tenth year, when he taught you the price of disobedience to a king! Now he knows you consort with the enemy and thanks me for my vigilance, rewards me with praise and beautiful things. I warned him that you would be trouble, that all your kind were dangerous—now he believes me, and you will have only darkness until you die."

The blade dug into his throat and Bran felt his own power in it, gleaming in the gold. He wanted to awaken it, to burn her with her proximity to a power she used but didn't understand—but she was human, not *sidhe*. His power might frighten her, but he didn't think it could hurt her.

Dealla spoke and her voice was low and greedy in Bran's ears.

"Do it, traitor, whatever it is you are thinking. Fight against me, so I have a chance to slay you now!"

Bran had never heard anyone sound as hungry for death as Dealla did at that moment. He felt a trickle of blood move wetly on his throat where the dagger had pierced his skin. It itched. He said nothing in response to Dealla's taunt, stood mute and still and stared down the blade of her sword, at her wild eyes. Dealla had never been kind, but had she always been mad like this?

Then she pushed herself back, away from and off him, and called to two of the guards.

"Aodhan! Cathal! Take him and bind him, we've spent too long at this already."

She focused her eyes on Bran.

"No ropes for you, *sidhe*. I know what will hold you, what will keep you weak."

Harsh hands closed tight around Bran's biceps. Dark chains of cold iron were passed around his wrists, and Bran felt more hands at his back shove him forward while the hands that held the chains pulled. The metal stung his skin and weighed on him. The power within him began to flicker and fade. He stumbled and fell and the king's guards dragged him along the rough road for several steps before Bran was able to get his feet under him again and lurch upright.

All at once he thought of Macsen and wondered, not for the first time that morning, where he had gone. Last night the Red King had promised forever, hadn't he? He'd been drunk as a lord, but...but no. It didn't matter whether he'd meant it or not. The way things were, Bran would be dead before the day was out. Even if he wasn't, Dealla would put him someplace even Macsen Cadoc couldn't find him.

If he comes back.

Bran stumbled again, but this time he caught himself before he could fall. He kept his gaze on Dealla, walking ten paces in front of him.

One day, that desire to kill, that mocking greed — one day, it was going to destroy her.

He hoped he was there to see it.

* * * *

Saoirse walked near the middle of the procession of guards, beside her sister. She clutched her new staff tightly in her hands, and watched a pair of guards drag Bran along behind her out of the corner of her eye. Occasionally, Saoirse looked up at her sister's face and the cruel smile she wore. More than once she turned to look at Bran as the contingent made its way down the road.

It wasn't a long way, but it curved beside the water where it came down from the hilltop and meandered through the village until it reached the palace at the river's great bend. When they came to the edge of the marketplace, people began to gather around and behind them, and Saoirse watched them with interest.

She was eight years old, but it was only in the last few months that she had been allowed to mingle in the village. Her earliest memories were not of friends or toys but training. She hadn't left the palace until she was seven, and her life was lessons and training. The lessons were about the kingdom that her father ruled and the responsibilities that would be hers as she grew older, a princess of his blood. The training was to prepare her for the fight that she inherited as a huntress, because she was a Milesian woman and because her sister said it was to be so.

She had had lessons about the danger that was the *sidhe*, too, about how the old fight, once ended, had broken out anew at the request of an allied king. *Sidhe.* She turned her eyes toward Bran again, then quickly away. Her sister was watching.

Sidhe...

Dealla had told her about the ancient bet that had bought their people the isle of Ireland for themselves, free from any intrusion. About how Amergin had sung a song so strong it had overwhelmed the magic that hid the shores of Ireland, and about how the oath that Summer's king had made had bound the *sidhe* with their own magic.

The oath had been enough to close the Irish barrows to the *sidhe*, to block up the paths that led to the land under the hill. How many times had she heard Dealla say it?

'Eight hidden kingdoms, two for each season, dark and light. Not all of them concern us. Bright Summer's people were our foe in ages past, but it is the Red King who troubles us now, the king of night's half of winter. We hunt him for our allies, for the sake of human safety, and he threatens us with creatures of the foulest darkness — never forget it, Saoirse!'

She hadn't. Never. She hadn't been allowed to, had known all along what her training was for. Every time one of the other huntresses went to fight on the eastern island she was told about their successes and their failures — their deaths.

Saoirse turned her head a little to one side and tracked her sister's movements out of the corner of one eye. Dealla wasn't watching her, so Saoirse turned a little more and looked back at Bran again. His expression was wary and resigned, his brow furrowed, his lips thin, his jaw rigid. She stared hard at him, searching for the truth Dealla said was hidden there, but she couldn't see it.

How was Bran Fionnan dangerous? He had been kind and polite to her, and he had made her such a beautiful staff — and he wasn't one of the Red Court! She had been told many times that their captive *sidhe* was one of Summer's people, bound by an oath like all his kin. Why was he in chains?

She was beginning to see the way a seed of fear could make hate grow. Saoirse watched an older woman come close and greet Dealla, and kept one eye on her sister and one eye on the village around them. Something was happening on the right side of the street, and behind their procession. There were people coming outside, leaving their bags and trades behind and following along in Dealla's wake. While Dealla spoke with the old women they weren't walking as fast, for which Saoirse was grateful, but that meant that the crowd was beginning to catch up.

In a minute or so, the people were all around them, the numbers still growing. Saoirse heard angry mutters that grew into a subdued roar through force of numbers. For the first time this morning, she was glad for the presence of her father's guards. Something splashed in front of her foot. What was it? A guard nudged her around whatever it was and spoke to her quietly, the first words any of them had said to her.

"Just keep moving, Princess, pay no attention. You're not their target, you'll be fine."

"Not...their target?"

She turned despite the guard's words, and saw that the crowd around them had begun to pelt Bran with refuse and stones. Wide eyed, she watched him walk without turning, without moving aside, without even raising his bound hands to shield his head. Saoirse followed a rock that cut Bran's shoulder back to the one who threw it—a man who made the best jewelry, Dealla was always buying things from him.

Saoirse had never seen him any way but red-faced and smiling, holding out even the simplest piece of work like a masterpiece. Once he had given her a piece of raw honeycomb for a treat while her sister shopped. Now his face was purple, contorted with anger — monstrous.

Eyes wide, Saoirse looked around her and saw other people, strangers and familiar faces, all of them the same, all of them changed. *Monsters.* Thus distracted, it was at the last second that the girl saw movement out of the corner of her eye and turned to face it. A stone!

Saoirse stopped dead, frozen in place. The sharp edges of the stone coming at her were clear in her vision, and she could already feel the pain — but it didn't come.

Somehow, Bran leaped and fell at the same time. He fell almost on top of her, between her and the stone. The guards were on in him in the next moment and a few of them kicked at him until he was able to get on his feet again. Saoirse saw only the bloody bruise on Bran's shoulder where the rock that had been meant for her had struck him. She met his eyes and saw them focus on her. Then he winced a little, rippled his shoulders in the faintest shrug, smiled and *winked* at her.

Tears welled up in her eyes. Why were they doing this? She knew Bran was good — she knew it — so why! She clenched her hands on the staff he had made for her. What was it he had said? She tried hard to remember, but only parts of it came back to her.

'This weapon is yours…it will protect you. Learn to handle it with skill. Power is more than…killing.'

Saoirse shook her head. She did know one thing for sure.

'Remember, I made it special, just for you.'

The girl looked back over her shoulder at Bran, then quickly forward again. Silently, she made a promise — an oath.

I swear, Bran Fionnan. I swear I'll remember, and I'll do what you said.

She felt a spark in her fingertips, where they touched the gold on the weapon. Then she looked up, distracted by a great slamming noise.

They were home. The palace doors were flung wide, and she saw her father standing at the entry to the great hall. He bore the same kind of awful smile that Dealla had worn all the way here, and Saoirse shied away from it. What was happening to everyone? Her father looked at Dealla and nodded once with a flicker of his usual smile. Then his face turned hard again and he spoke to the guards.

"Two of you bring the traitor into the hall. The rest of you are dismissed, you've all done well."

Saoirse avoided her father's eye, and thus a similar dismissal. When no one was looking, she slipped behind the pair of guards dragging Bran behind her sister, and hid in the shadows at the back of the great hall.

* * * *

Bran stayed where he was when the guards who were pulling him dropped his chains and left him. He heard the king dismiss them, sending them out of the room, but the words came through a roar and Bran's heartbeat pounded in his ears. *Danger, the worst danger.* This was the feeling he should have had in Macsen's presence but hadn't, the feeling that his life could end at any moment.

Dealla came close to him and stared up at his face. Her eyes were open windows to him, and he saw cruelty at the heart of her and a fanatic hatred for that which was not like her. That loathing was focused on him because she thought of all *sidhe* as nothing more than dangerous animals, and yet could see nothing but a shape of perfect, gleaming manhood when she looked at him.

Just for her, Bran crafted a smile that told her he knew exactly what she was looking for and what she had seen instead. The crust of blood dried at the corner of his mouth peeled painfully with the curve of his lips, but he didn't care. No insult he could have spoken would have struck her more sharply than a smile like this one, a smile that said he knew he was nothing like her and didn't want to be. A smile that said nothing she did could hurt him because of that. He saw it hit home, watched her eyes narrow and darken. The muscles of her face twitched with rage. Then, because he knew it would bother her, Bran looked past Dealla as if she wasn't there and peered up at her father instead.

"So here I am again. Will you tell me why, or does the sword come for me?"

Dealla's knife flashed into her hand before he had finished his sentence.

"Beast! Silence yourself before our king!"

Bran turned to look back at her. The dagger in her hand gleamed cold with gold. He knew that blade — he had made it, like all the other weapons like it. It struck him suddenly that she was threatening him with a weapon he had made himself, imbued with his own power. In a flash of movement Bran reached forward and caught Dealla's dagger in the chains that hung heavy from his wrists. He wrapped them twice around the gleaming metal and yanked her close to him, until they were face to face.

"Your father is *your* king, Dealla. Not mine!"

He shoved her backward without unwinding the chain, and she cried out and fell back. The knife was ripped from her hands and dangled in Bran's bonds, but he didn't try to take it. The king's guards were a moment's call away, and the king himself was standing in front of him, watching, apparently amused by his daughter's discomfiture but still with a hand on the hilt of his sword.

Bran relaxed his arms and let the knife fall out of the chains. It hit the ground with a dull thud, and he met Dealla's eyes with a hard stare.

"Don't think I'll let you use the weapons I made against me, human."

Then, once more, he looked up at her father's face. He addressed the king by name, something he had never dared do before. He felt oddly free, as if now, facing the ultimate consequence, he could do anything without fear. His blood felt hot. The power, the pressure within him that he usually disregarded was an inferno in his body. He knew there was fire in his eyes, could see the gold glowing through his skin.

For the first time, he didn't feel like he needed or wanted to restrain it.

"You haven't answered, Cáelbad mac Briuin. Is it the sword for me?"

Mac Briuin laughed a little, then shook his head and tightened his fist around the hilt of his own weapon despite his words.

"No, traitor, I don't intend to slay you yet. Not until you tell me what is it that you have to do with one of our enemy."

Bran stayed silent.

"Come now—I know you're one of Summer's people. I thought that made you tame—or has Dealla been right all along? Are you as dangerous as the fiends of the Red Court?"

"How could I say? Did you forget that you stole me when I was only a child? That I don't know anything about what it means to be *sidhe* because of you?" Bran scowled and shook his head. "No, I don't think you've forgotten."

Mac Briuin's smile began to slip. "It would have been better for you to never know what you were, but it was not something that could be hidden. Not when it was your power that we stole you for. Now, despite being watched and raised so carefully, I find that you still want to be more like those creatures!"

"Stop insulting what you don't understand!"

Bran's words snapped across Mac Briuin's voice like a whip, and the man finally gave up the struggle to keep a pleasant expression on his face.

"You intend to keep your silence? To protect the one who came to you, maybe? I warn you, it won't be easy for you if you do—"

"I think we both know how this is going to end either way."

Mac Briuin took two steps down from his throne. "Be reasonable, traitor. Your punishment doesn't need to end your life."

Bran grinned grimly. If he was going to die, he wasn't going to be afraid—it wouldn't be on his knees, or begging for anything. Not from these people, not from this man!

"That implies I *have* a life, here among you people. I'm not like you, and you know it—ha! Know it. It terrifies you! I don't belong here, Cáelbad mac Briuin! I never have."

Mac Briuin's face changed. Bran didn't know if it was the loss of his smile that had caused it or if the king had just grown tired of playing nice. Whatever it was, his expression grew hard and dark. Like the old bronze images of the ancient kings, Mac Briuin's eyes stared into Bran's face. His downturned mouth drew deep, shadowed lines in his face. He drew his sword, and held it point first before him. There was no gold on it, only hard steel, wet and red as if with blood in the light of the torches beside the throne.

"You dare show such disrespect, here, standing before me? You dare to speak my name, you dare to defy me? Did you not learn your lesson the first time you stood against me, Rud?"

Bran stepped forward, slowly, dragging his chains with him. He went so far as to step up two stairs on the way to the dais and the throne on top of it. He stopped only because Mac Briuin was standing above him, the point of his sword pressed against Bran's breast.

Bran stood still and confronted the king with his presence, dared the man to run him through. The pressure of his body against the tip of the king's blade drew a bead of blood that ran down his chest, and when he spoke his voice was low and cold.

"Don't call me *Rud*. My name is Bran Fionnan, and I am not like you. I'm not human. I belong anywhere else. Not with you Milesians — not even among men. I belong with Macsen Cadoc more than with you — I should have gone with him when he asked."

Bran tightened his hands into fists.

"I should have defied you long ago, but I was young and stupid then and I didn't know what it was that you would ask of me, I didn't know what this life would really be like!"

He felt the weight of the chains on his wrists, but they were no heavier than the weight of everything that had come before. Loneliness, the making of terrible weapons, the fear and the promise of pain...of death. If it had come for him, he would take it on his own terms.

"I'll say it again, for the last time. You aren't my king. I have no life here with your kind. You know as well as I do there's nothing human about me."

Mac Briuin's frown became a smile, but it was an ugly smile. "Yes, I know. I know, and now I understand my daughter's concern. You were right, Dealla! There was never anything worth trusting here. Do you understand, traitor? Someone has always been watching. *Always.* Since the moment we knew that you were aware of what you were, there have always been eyes on you. Eyes watching you work, wander, try to escape—ah, but you could never find the secret ways to the hidden kingdom, could you?"

Bran felt a pulse of pain and rage. He heard Dealla's footsteps cross behind him, then felt her yank on the trailing length of chain. Her tug pulled him backward down the stairs. He fell painfully onto his back and let out a sharp breath but no cry. He stared up at her, murderous thoughts in his mind. He had never wanted to kill a person before but this woman, this *human!*

Dealla spoke and her voice was like ice in his ears. "I warned you, Father. The barrows of our land have been shut for a thousand years by the pact between our ancestors and Summer's people. When we crossed into Summer's kingdom and took this creature twenty years ago, that pact was broken. Only the likelihood that Summer's people had ceased seeking a way through the closed barrows long ago protects us."

Bran watched Dealla bend and pick up her blade.

"I can't deny that the work this traitor has done has been useful, but I have never agreed that we needed him. I have never thought it was wise that we provoked the *sidhe* with such a theft—one such enemy is enough, and for the sake of your *allies* on the eastern island we have made such an enemy in the Red King."

She came and stood over Bran and grasped the chains again.

"But it's too late to worry about that. Shall I kill him, Father? I could do it with words, or with steel—I *want* to slay him, Father, I want to—"

"No, Dealla. We discussed this."

"Then allow me to restrain the beast at least!"

Bran heard their words and frowned in confusion. They had *discussed* him? Was he to serve some other, worse purpose than what they had already demanded of him? He was sure he would find out soon enough and less sure that he wanted to.

Mac Briuin must have nodded at his daughter's question, because Dealla turned back to look down at Bran with pleasure on her face. The man didn't speak and Bran couldn't see him through his daughter. Her hands dragged the chain into shorter loops and held them tightly. She spoke words in a slow, rhythmic voice, neither speech nor song, something in-between—old words, old magic.

"Red the blood
that lies between us
like the hart's blood
sprayed on the bracken —
By the red blood, I bind you!

Cold the wind
That binds the bird-wings

summons the winter,
wind of winter to freeze you –
Like the birds, I bind you!"

The words were power, power that Bran could see. Magic flowered in the air, carried on Dealla's breath, and light that was deep crimson and glacial pale entwined and moved in sharp, bright streamers, wrapping around Bran's flesh. He *felt* the cold she spoke of, felt a surge of chill ride his pulse and sink into his blood until it encompassed his whole body. He struggled, but it took only a moment before he was rendered motionless.

The smile on her face as she hovered above him was colder than the spell. Dealla's voice came slow and blistering to Bran's ears through the chill of the enchantment.

"Do you see, traitor? I am more than just a huntress. I carry the blood of kings and all the ancient songs of power are mine! I am witch and warrior both, and when it is time for you to die, I am the one who will kill you!"

Bran heard Mac Briuin speak then, like a man calling a dog off a bone.

"Enough now, Dealla."

She dropped Bran and turned back to her father. Bran hit the floor at an awkward angle and lay where he had fallen, frozen in place. Despite the fact that his muscles were dead and useless, he still felt pain. He tried to distract himself by focusing on Dealla's argument with her father, even if listening to her beg for permission to kill him was less than pleasant.

"He's dangerous, Father. Don't you understand? I don't think anything holds the *sidhe* back now. I don't think the oath has enforced the closing of the barrows since we brought this creature out of the mound! And if the thing that's been visiting him goes to see Summer's Queen, the Red Court might lead Summer's people back to Ireland!"

"It won't happen, Dealla. You're forgetting that the Red Court and Summer's people have been at war for ages. There's nothing but bad feeling between them. That's how we knew taking the traitor would be of help to us — they can slay each other, those monsters, even when we can't do a thing."

"My huntresses have failed three times now to kill the Red King. If one like him comes seeking the traitor —"

"If one like him comes seeking, he does so at his own peril. Fighting one of your women sent alone on a hunt is different from facing all of them together. Enough, Dealla. I told you before, I won't change my mind. The traitor will die for a purpose. There are many sacrifices that might be strengthened by the blood of a *sidhe*."

Dealla's voice grew more strident, and Bran felt renewed chill that had nothing to do with the spell that bound him.

"The priests won't like it, Father. The church will protest, and you know that our allies —"

"Do I care for the words of a few men in coarse cloth, Daughter? Do I care for the thoughts of allies who flee in fear from such as this traitor, even as they beg us to stand and fight? No — I am king in more than name, and I will do as I think is best. Our gods are older than the Roman priests' God — and vengeful."

Dealla bowed, and Bran saw the contortion of her father's face, rigid with fury and pride over the bending of her back.

"As you will it, Father."

"Yes. As I will it. How long will this binding you've placed on the traitor hold?"

"Until the sun of spring melts the winter ice, if you wish."

Mac Briuin laughed but the sound was unpleasant.

"It need not last so long as that. Go, bring guards and a cage for him. Something big enough for him to stand and move in but small enough to fit on the dais—I want this traitor beside my throne as proof of the submission of the *sidhe* that our ancestors won. He will serve as evidence of our ascendance for any visitor to see."

Dealla bowed again, and left. Bran followed her with his ears until his attention was jerked back to Mac Briuin by the man's hand on his tunic, pulling him upright. He stared down into Bran's eyes with an unyielding fury, with the same cruel gleam that had tinted Dealla's vision.

"Rud, *sidhe*, Summer's son—from this moment until the moment you die, the only name you will bear is *traitor*. No song will remember you, and no one will speak of you again. You dare to say you are beyond my authority, my power?"

Once, twice, the king drove his fist into Bran's face. Through the cold of the binding that held him, Bran felt the pain of the blows like melting heat, but he still couldn't move. Then Mac Briuin dropped him, and Bran lay where he had fallen, breathless, his head ringing.

"At first I thought you were just a fool, that you'd chosen unwisely for a lover—that maybe you wanted companionship of your own kind. It was known to me that you did not go seeking out your visitor, that he came to you and that you fought him the first night...haven't I made clear that everything you do is known to me? I could have offered you a kindness, I could have looked the other way, but tonight you have proved yourself true to the nature my daughter claims is yours."

Mac Briuin leaned close to Bran's face.

"Do you know how glad I am that I listened to my daughter? I know the name you spoke, traitor. I know the name of Macsen Cadoc. It is always wise to know one's enemies, is it not?"

Bran's eyes widened in horror.

Reckless, reckless, I was too reckless, so stupid, of course he knows that name!

Mac Briuin lifted his lip, a sneer and a grimace of satisfaction. "You aren't just a traitor, you are dangerous — consorting with the Red King! You'd lead him and his court right to me. You'd see all of us dead, my kingdom in flames — I won't have it!"

Bran could only stare. The man was mad! Bran only wanted to get away, to live out his life somewhere no one would ever ask him to forge a weapon again.

Never again.

Some peace and quiet, that was what he wanted — and now maybe Macsen, too.

Except I won't see you again, will I? Red King.

"You'll pay the price for your actions, traitor! I'll make sure of that."

Mac Briuin's voice was black with rage. Out of the corner of one eye, Bran saw a booted foot come toward him, but he *still* couldn't move. A surge of frustration rushed through him, but he could only watch the blow come toward him.

The kick struck him in the temple and he knew nothing but the penetrating cold that followed him into unconsciousness.

Chapter Five

When Bran woke, it was to pain and darkness, silence and bars. Night had come, and he was relieved to find that the spell Dealla had bound him with was gone. A little at a time, every movement slow, Bran stretched cramped muscles and tried to rub some life into his limbs. Bruises had blossomed like purple flowers beneath his skin, painful in many places. His head ached, and when he tried to rub his aching temple he hissed with pain and had to stop. Cáelbad mac Briuin had a heavy kick.

Bran paced back and forth in his cage, trying to work some of the soreness from his legs. He could take two steps in any direction, but that was all. After a while he lay flat on his back in the center of the thing and closed his eyes. There was dirt under his back, no floor to the cage, but the bars and top of it were iron.

"I'm such an idiot." He rubbed his hands over his face and let out a heavy sigh. "Completely stupid... What was I thinking? Not that anything I said isn't true."

The burning feeling that had supported him earlier, given him strength for defiance, was gone now. Bran scowled and winced when muscles that shouldn't be tightening screamed at him in protest. He felt the cut at the corner of his lip split open again, and pressed the back of his hand against his mouth. The taste of blood reminded him of Macsen, and he closed his eyes.

"Macsen Cadoc. Ha. I should never have said your name."

He scowled again and this time didn't bother about the pain. He should have known — would have, if he'd been thinking, if he'd stayed calm like he'd promised himself he would as they'd dragged him away from his house. Hells, nothing Mac Briuin had said was as bad as those fools in the street throwing things at him. He sat back on the floor and lay flat, hands folded beneath his head. Aching, tired and alone with his thoughts, Bran fell into a restless sleep.

The dream was ice, and a view of a forest — a view of a winter night. Bran felt his gaze shift back and forth, and as it did so Bran recognized that this was not his view or his being. He was someone else, had opened a door to another consciousness, but it didn't seem strange to him. It was a dream, after all. He looked down at his hands, and they weren't his hands, and that didn't distress him. He even knew whose hands they were.

Macsen Cadoc.

As if in echo, he heard a pleasing rumble.

"Bran Fionnan…I am already tired of waiting, already missing you."

The view shifted wildly, and Bran saw a stranger standing at the entrance to the chamber. A woman? No, not a woman. *Sidhe.* Her mouth moved, but Bran couldn't hear her speaking. He could only hear Macsen's voice, sharper now, irritated.

"I've no need of you—"

He waved her away, but the *sidhe*-woman came closer and Bran learned her name because Macsen said it, petulant. The Red King's voice held a child's anger at being disobeyed.

"I said to leave me, Talaith!"

Bran couldn't be unhappy. Macsen was brooding over him. Missing him, as he was himself missed. Bran admitted that to himself easily—that he missed Macsen Cadoc, that he wanted him to be near. It was easier to be honest in a dream.

The view shifted to Talaith's mouth as Macsen turned his head, and Bran felt Macsen heave a sigh and turn to face the female completely. He spoke with some aggravation.

"The red tunic—no, a gold one. And no more pets. Feed them to the guards if you want, I don't need them anymore."

Bran burned with pleasure to hear those words, and he wondered—was this a real thing? Was Macsen thinking of him? Would Macsen come looking for him, find him here and take him away?

I should have agreed to go with you, Macsen. Why didn't you just take me?

"Bran Fionnan—Bran Fionnan, are you awake?"

A girl's voice, incongruous, broke open the surface of Bran's dream, shattered it like a fragile eggshell. Bran sat up quickly, too quickly, then steadied himself on his hands and blinked.

The darkness wasn't the same as it had been when he'd fallen asleep, it was warm with some presence now. He blinked, and peered, wishing he had the clear, bright sight Macsen had in his dream. He accepted that dream as if he knew it was real, without even thinking about it. That place—it was a real place, had to be. And Macsen—

But Bran heard the voice again then, faintly plaintive, and knew who had woken him from that dream.

"Bran—Bran Fionnan?"

Bran answered in a low voice, "Saoirse Saorla. I'm awake, Princess."

She stepped forward a few steps, and a gleam of moonlight highlighted her hair, lit the amber stone in the band that still bound it back from her forehead. Bran smiled at her, but only faintly. It was too much to hope that she would be different than those who had raised and trained her. He didn't have the strength for hopes like that.

He was pleasantly surprised when she came forward and pressed herself against the bars of the cage.

"I couldn't get the key, Bran Fionnan, I'll keep trying, though. Here—can you reach? I brought water, and food—Father didn't notice that I didn't eat mine, he never pays any attention to me, and Dealla was too busy bragging about...well, about you."

The girl's words were swift and soft and full of apology. She spoke her sister's name with some venom, and Bran stood up and crossed to sit by the bars in front of her. Saoirse held out a water skin and Bran drank deeply before he took the apple she passed to him and the joint of some wild bird.

The grease and the salt stung his cut lips, but he was hungry enough not to care. It was only with food in front of him that Bran remembered he'd never eaten breakfast, or even dinner the night before. Saoirse took the bones back from him in exchange for half a loaf of bread and stowed them in her leather satchel.

Bran devoured the bread to crumbs and took the water skin back from her gratefully. When his thirst was quenched, he dribbled a little of the liquid on the hem of his tunic and used it to wipe away some of the blood crusting his face. Then he gave the skin back to her and settled himself against the bars.

"Thank you, Princess."

"Why do you call me that? You said Father's not your king, so—"

"Heard that, huh? Well, you aren't your father, Saoirse Saorla. You are so little like him that I hardly believe you're a daughter of his blood."

The girl stood then and stuck her arms through the bars and hugged Bran tightly.

"I'm sorry—I'm sorry that my father's bad, and Dealla—"

Surprised, touched, Bran reached out a hand and patted her shoulder with an awkward movement.

"It's not for you to worry about, Princess."

Her hair tickled him as she shook her head. She pulled back from him and he saw stubbornness printed on her face.

"It *is*. It *is* for me to worry about! Or I'm not a princess—I'm just a...a...I'm just like Dealla!"

She hugged him again, and this time he was ready for it.

"I won't let you be a sacrifice, Bran Fionnan. I know you're good even if you are *sidhe*."

Bran blinked. "You—listened to that, too?"

She nodded. "I heard *everything*."

Bran caught a noise then, and the girl must have too. She started back from him, gasped then turned back for only a moment.

"The guards are coming! There's a feast tomorrow night, I'll be able to get more food for you, so I'll come back when it's over. Don't...don't say anything back to Father when he talks, or he'll hurt you worse. He said so, after supper."

Bran didn't have the heart to tell her that her father would probably hurt him worse regardless. He only nodded, and she rewarded him with a brilliant smile.

Saoirse turned and fled into the shadows. After a moment, he could no longer hear her, and when the door of the hall opened and a pair of guards peered in, there was only Bran, sitting alone in the center of his cage. They turned and left after only a moment, just long enough to see that Bran was still there. When they were gone, he saw Saoirse's little figure slip forward and grasp hold of the edge of the door as it was closing.

She stopped for a moment and turned to wave back at him. Then she was gone, and for reasons he couldn't even begin to contemplate, Bran felt...reassured. Warmer, now.

Saoirse Saorla, huh?

So maybe there was hope, after all. But a feast...

Bran looked around, imagined the empty darkness full of tables and people, voices and food. He shuddered, and pulled himself back away from the bars to the center of the cage.

"It's going to get worse."

* * * *

The next day passed slowly, and Bran learned new definitions of boredom as he sat without speaking, and waited for something horrible to happen.

The feast Saoirse had warned him about was far worse than even the worst things Bran had imagined. As if he were an animal in a cage, men poked and prodded at him with the butts of their spears, or dared each other drunkenly to risk a *sidhe* curse and touch him. He said nothing when Dealla proclaimed a second victory over the *sidhe* and offered him as proof, said nothing even when Mac Briuin announced that Bran would be sacrificed at Imbolc, the festival of rebirth celebrating the end of winter. What was there for him to say?

Dealla sat on the dais beside her father, on a high chair set at his right hand. From his place at Mac Briuin's left, he could just barely see her, but Saoirse wasn't beside her. Bran distracted himself from crude words and painful prodding by searching for the girl with his eyes. He finally caught sight of her seated at one of the high tables, beside a woman who shared the green of her eyes and the shape of her nose. Her mother, maybe? Bran didn't know. He hadn't seen her before.

Saoirse looked up then and met his eyes, smiled at him—was she so happy, because he wasn't talking like he had promised? But no, it wasn't a happy smile. *Courage*, it said. She was only eight years old, just a girl-child, the daughter of his enemy, but he took comfort from her regardless. So what if she was just a child? He wasn't alone here, and that was something.

When the feasting was done and the hall was empty and silent, the warriors dispersed and Bran found himself looking forward to the visit the girl had promised.

It was late when Saoirse returned, mouse-quiet, and this time Bran had already woken from another strange, dim dream of Macsen Cadoc. Like the dream of the night before, it was slippery in his waking consciousness even as he remembered that it had been clear and perfect while he was asleep. Bran remembered only the feeling that Macsen was thinking of him and the knowledge that he had been outside himself. And maybe snow — *snow...*

Bran's skin tingled with coolness. He shook his head to clear it and greeted the girl standing before him. Saoirse had brought a much smaller version of the feast with her, boar and mutton, bread and berries and a leather satchel of stewed vegetables, cold and messy but delicious — even a little cake, glistening with honey in the faint gleam of the moonlight. He saw the girl staring at it, and grinned, wondered what it had cost her to put that away for him.

When Bran had eaten everything else he took the cake in his hand and broke it in two. He passed one half back through the bars to the girl.

"Here, Princess. Share with me."

"You're sure, Bran Fionnan?"

He nodded and hid the widening of his smile. She was already reaching out to take it. Bran settled himself on the ground again with a wince that he hoped he hid, then turned a serious expression in Saoirse's direction.

"You should be careful, you know. If you're caught helping me, you'll get in trouble. Not that I'm not grateful — "

Saoirse smiled, her lips sticky with crumbs and shiny honey.

"I know — but I'm good at sneaking. I get away from Dealla when we go down to the village, sometimes, it's easy. She doesn't tell 'cause she'd get in trouble. Things are the same at home — Father's too busy to bother with me, and Mother doesn't care what I do so it's only the guards I have to watch out for."

Her quiet, lisping voice fell silent for a moment. He saw her tilt her head, listening, then shake it.

"Do you want more water, Bran Fionnan?"

"Just call me Bran, Princess. Just Bran. And yes, please."

She handed him the skin.

* * * *

Macsen Cadoc returned to his kingdom with dawn's light chasing his heels, drained by the sun he had run through. He sank into his throne and closed his eyes, and it seemed like the next moment he was dreaming. It was of Bran, waking tousled in the same position Macsen had left him in, and Macsen was confused.

He knew these were bits and pieces of the waking life of Bran Fionnan, but he hadn't been expecting anything like this tonight. It wasn't Samhain any longer and he'd never had visions of Bran any other time. The events of Bran's morning flashed past him, disturbed by the uneven way they were perceived.

Macsen woke slowly, agitated and uncertain. Sleep and the images it had brought him clung to his consciousness, and Macsen shook his head and pressed the heels of his hands against his eyes.

"Bran Fionnan, what...are you doing? A palace...a girl...and a king? And you...hmm."

He couldn't remember. The old dreams were bright in his mind, but this new one felt...sluggish. A lance of pain struck Macsen's temple as the memory slipped out of his grasp, but it faded quickly. He stretched and stood. Phantom aches dissipated and the cloud of sleep that had fogged his brain dispersed.

Macsen crossed his chamber and looked out his window across the winter forest. The dark horizon was visible through the leafless trees beyond the palace orchards, and above it the shimmering moon as it changed, passing through its mortal phases. A month in the mortal world was a single day of night here, and the hours were marked by the changing shape of the midnight moon.

The view, bright and sharp as it was, failed to calm Macsen like it usually did. Within him something of Bran brushed at his consciousness like a loose thread tickling the back of his neck. Macsen did his best to disregard it, but the feeling wouldn't be ignored. It was like he had come home to find that something precious had been stolen from him...only nothing was missing.

He looked down at his hands, clenched his fists tightly then relaxed them just as fast.

"Bran Fionnan..."

"My lord, you are awake."

Macsen turned abruptly and saw Talaith standing in the door. He said nothing, only glared at her, and she smiled.

"I'll bring your clothes, my lord –"

"Don't bother, I've no need of you."

Macsen waved her away, but she was no more obedient now than she usually was and came to stand beside him instead of going away. He glared at her, but it was no good. She knew he wouldn't do anything to her, not after eight hundred years. *Such a pity.*

"My lord, the crimson or the green tunic? Please choose one, you won't like whatever I pick. And the girl you drank for the Samhain sacrifice, which of your pets do you wish to replace her? There's a black-haired boy who's lovely, and a girl from the south—"

Macsen gritted his teeth and whipped around to look at Talaith again, sharp words on his tongue, but she was looking back at him with a placid expression, amusement in her eyes. Macsen held back his retort and answered her questions. Maybe then she would *go away*?

"The red tunic—no, a gold one. And no more pets. Feed them to the guards if you want, I don't need them anymore."

Talaith appeared surprised, but she nodded and bowed slightly—only slightly. Macsen turned away from her as she left and this time he looked, not out at the forests, but down at the dance. Color and light lapped at the edges of his vision, motion synchronized to the throbbing sound of the ancient drums.

The rhythm was strong as a heartbeat, pulsed with a familiar pressure. *Bran*. The taste of his kiss, his blood, his skin, were clear in Macsen's memory. He licked his lips and closed his eyes. His hunger, his thirst, was for Bran…his thoughts were fixated on Bran, even with the presence of the great dance. He seemed close…but perhaps that was just the memory of the dream.

Talaith returned with her arms full of gold silk and said nothing to him this time. Macsen watched her leave tunic and trousers on his bed, but he was grateful that she didn't make him speak. His teeth felt sharp in his mouth, and though the thirst within him had not yet raised its ravaging head, the violence that came with it was loose in him, seeking a target. *Why?*

He didn't know. Restless aggression, undirected aggression…it set him on edge. He felt like he was waiting and shouldn't be, but couldn't think for what. He wanted to sleep so that he could return to the presence he longed for, and he wanted to join the mad urgency of the dance. Macsen shook himself, and tried to suppress the wild thing moving within him. He dressed, then went down among his people.

The dancers made a circle that touched the edge of the clearing, in front of the great tree in which was his palace, and before which was the dais that held his throne. There were circles within circles, spirals turning in upon themselves, then outward. *Sidhe* of many kinds held out their hands, their claws, their shimmering wings, their gossamer fingers, reached with many filaments of form and being.

They became one great whirlwind, endless in their motion and their magic. They were the whistle of the night's winds and the spaces between the stars, but they were just as much the stars themselves. They were the flickering firelight and the shadows that brightness cast, and they were the heart-pounding excitement of the dance itself.

For an endless time, a night and a sunless day in that shadowed realm, the Red King gave in to his own nature, gave up his heart to the raving sound of the flutes and drums. He tried to spend his urgent energy in the festival and its madness. The feeling inside him that was most moving was new to him, and deep, a feeling wrapped up in the name that haunted his lips even here in the dance where he had no soul, no single consciousness.

Bran Fionnan.

There was heat in Macsen Cadoc, instead of the ice that had always ruled him, but by the time the moon had gone through its shifting phases, Macsen had grown still within himself. The wildness was quiet, and only the feeling remained. The name of it was as hot in him as the memory of the sounds Bran had made becoming his lover.

"My...lover. I asked him, didn't I?"

It struck him then that he had never had a lover before, not in a thousand years. There were many he had seduced for the sake of pleasure, and the act of seduction was itself a part of his nature—part of the hunter in him. Yet it was only ever bodies in motion, flesh seeking its own ends...that was not the same as taking a lover. Not when words were power and there was no word more dangerous than love.

Was that the feeling? Want was not enough, but *need*—to need someone, was that love? To need them near you every moment, as he needed Bran—to have them in your thoughts, your dreams, your everything? A feeling and more than a feeling. A state of being...a state of soul.

Macsen smiled to himself and went up out of the noise toward the dais. He passed by the hands that reached for him from among the dancers, ignored the voices calling out his name, beckoning him back. He mounted the steps to his silent throne, leaned his head on his hand and looked down at his court.

"It's love I feel for you, Bran Fionnan... What do I do about that?"

He couldn't stand the thought of rejection, of being turned away. There was a tingle of unease when he thought about what might happen if his Summer prince said no. Would the power of the oath that had kept him from taking Bran away with him act again? Could it keep him from seeking his lover out if he said he didn't want him?

"Perhaps if I wait, when I go to him he'll be so wild with longing he'll say yes to anything. Perhaps...yes.

Like the first time, it will make him want me more when I return. It can't do any harm."

Time passed, and Macsen fell into a shallow doze.

* * * *

From within the cage that barred his world, Bran tracked the moon as it waxed and waned overhead. He kept track of time by the shape of the moon when he could see it and watched the daylight brighten and fade through chinks in the walls and ceiling of the windowless hall.

His days were darker and emptier than his nights. At night, he was occasionally visited by Saoirse. Bran saved his strength so that he had a smile ready in case she came, and the nights she didn't were the worst. There was no distraction then, and he would spend the black hours warring within himself until dawn poured over the edge of the sky.

Those nights, he wondered about Saoirse and if she had been caught, and about Macsen and if he would really return. When his doubts were at their worst, the cage around him seemed like the only proof that he had ever felt Macsen's hands on him, ever tasted the Red King's kiss.

Then he would dream, and wake, and for a moment have Macsen's presence so fresh in his mind that it was all he could do not to scream.

In the beginning, Bran tried not to wait. He tried to put thoughts like *Red King* and *save me* out of his mind, tried to be logical about his chances and accept his death. Despite himself, Bran clung to his dreams and the little of them he could remember upon waking.

He clung to the promise of them and the way Macsen always seemed to be thinking of him, and he clung to them because it was only in those dreams that he was free from fear in all its various forms. He showed those fears to no one—not to the huntresses and guards who ridiculed him, not to the king who taunted him, not to the girl who risked punishment to visit him at night. He couldn't stand the thought of showing weakness to his tormentors, and Saoirse…Saoirse was too young to help him shoulder his pain. Only the dreams made it less.

The shortest night came and went and the solstice feasts with it, and in the deep cold that followed, Bran grew depressed and anxious and angry by turns. After midwinter, Saoirse's visits became more infrequent. Bran thought she might have been caught out of bed, because for at least a fortnight there was no sign of her. She didn't visit him at night, and she wasn't in the hall during meals, or even in passing—but then one night, unexpected, she came back to stand shivering in front of him with her precious little gifts.

Her movements were stiff and pained for many days after that, and Saoirse came to see him almost every night for nearly a week. Bran wondered if she'd been beaten for her transgression, but she said nothing when he asked. The way the girl smiled at him and changed the subject stuck in his memory.

Bran spent as much of his time as he could asleep. There was nothing else for him to do, and he wanted his dreams of Macsen and the strange court he could catch glimpses of through Macsen's eyes. He remembered more, the more he envisioned and sometimes even when he wasn't sleeping Bran would lay still and let his thoughts fill with images.

He saw a wide winter forest, snowbound, silent, its stillness broken by the falling of snow or the changing of the moon or the leaping of a white hart across the shadow of evergreens. They showed him glistening lights numerous as leaves hung from the naked boughs of trees, a steaming orchard set incongruous against the snow, and treasures that gleamed in the cold starlight of a moonless hour.

The dreams showed him Macsen. Macsen, waking alone in a circular chamber in a great bed, Macsen dressing in bright silk, Macsen stalking across the whiteness of his realm. They showed him Macsen muttering to himself, thinking of Bran, moving restlessly down from his dark throne to mingle with his court. They showed him Macsen dancing, wild movement in perfect rhythm, spinning and darting among the circles of other dancers. There were many visions of that dance, one long wildness that seemed to go on, and on, and on, until Bran lost himself in it the way Macsen seemed to have done and only woke when Saoirse called his name.

Bran had no way of knowing how much of what he saw was real, but the sensations were real, the *feelings* were real, and after a time the truth ceased to matter. The dreams were all he had to eat away the empty hours, and after a while, he wanted them because he wanted to see Macsen more than because he wanted time to pass.

A little at a time, he was learning Macsen's nature. Bran grew to see Macsen's arrogance as brash confidence, became acquainted with his cutting intelligence and with his power. Bran learned that Macsen was moody, sometimes grim, that his humor was always macabre and that he kept few companions. Those were the faces Bran grew familiar with because they were always nearby when Macsen needed them — like the female, Talaith.

Most of his time, Macsen spent alone. He was the Red King, and his status separated him even from his kin. The more Bran grew to understand him, the more he saw in Macsen a loneliness he was acquainted with, the loneliness he had lived with himself. That discovery fed warm feelings within him, the feelings tied to his desire that were not desire — unfamiliar emotions, comforting and painful.

Bran wondered most often if it was love, and thought it might be but couldn't tell. What did he know about love? It was only a dream, after all — and in any case it was unlikely he would ever see Macsen again. It had been two months already, wasn't that long enough that he could give up?

As the nights began to shorten again, and the moon passed through its second full cycle of phases since Bran's imprisonment, hope began to seem like a waste of energy. Sometimes he closed his eyes and wished he'd provoked Dealla enough the day she'd come for him that she'd just killed him instead of caging him like this — but whenever he thought that, the same words would come to him, every time.

'Mine, all mine, Bran Fionnan, mine forever — forever, all...all mine...'

They were the last words he'd heard from Macsen Cadoc and they haunted him. A pretty promise, even if it didn't mean anything in the end.

"What'd I think it was going to mean? His forever — ha. Like he'd come back for me when I already gave him what he wanted."

Memories of flesh and lust failed to warm him despite their heat.

"Anyway, it's too late now even if he did come. It was too late the moment they put me here. Even *he* couldn't fight Mac Briuin and all Ireland's huntresses by himself."

Two months became three, but that tiny ember of hope stayed alive inside Bran, promising, always promising—saying every morning to wait for the night. Some days Bran found he hated that hope, and some days he loved it, but either way, he knew who was to blame for it.

"It's your fault, Macsen Cadoc. All your fault."

As the third month of his imprisonment began to pass Bran by, one day at a time, he stopped wondering how long defiance could sustain him. He promised himself every day that it would be just a little bit longer, but deep inside himself he knew the truth, despite the fact that he had no real count of days.

Imbolc was coming, the night of the old sacrifice, the night on which men performed rites that promised death and rebirth. Bran had seen the rituals before, had sat at the outskirts of the dancing and the feasts. He had seen the red blood spilled from the sacrifice — a lamb, it had been. He had heard the old men complaining that the fields had been richer in the days before the priests of the Christ had come and started preaching for their god.

In the days when the sacrifice had not been the half-hearted gift of a beast but the sacrifice of a living man.

Bran wondered what they thought his blood would buy them.

It certainly hadn't done anything for him.

* * * *

Terror. Fading terror.

Macsen Cadoc knew it was a dream just by the feeling. It was all that possessed him — vulnerability, and terror. Had he ever felt fear? No! And surely not terror — what kind of memory...what kind of dream was this? *Cacophony.*

He was subjected to a madness of noise and human sounds. His ears beat with the closeness of it. He felt pain — faint, echoing, like the phantom sensations that had woken him from his dream of the day before. Dark wood crossed his vision, and Macsen saw a point on it, felt sharpness grate against his ribs —

But not his ribs. The inner awareness of the truth shocked the dream into sharp outlines, and he knew that he was seeing through Bran's eyes again.

My Bran, what is this?

The view shifted, and Macsen looked directly forward, past familiar hands and arms to black iron bars. Macsen knew only that it was Bran — that something was happening — something unspeakable.

Macsen's elbow slipped from the arm of his throne, and he jerked into wakefulness. The sense of abiding terror and the feeling that something was wrong, horribly wrong, remained with him. He sat upright and peered out across the court, past the dancers — nothing was there but the trees, moving in a cold wind Memory was hot within him — could it be real? And what of what he had seen the day before?

They had met now, they had touched, and more than touched. Would that have made the bond between them stronger? He didn't know, but it was so easy to connect the two things together.

"And I know your name, Bran Fionnan. I know your name and a name is power."

Macsen tried to sort his memories of the newest dreams, but he could sense that the order was wrong, the chronology...off. Black iron bars—a girl and a staff. The gleam of amber in the light of dawn and the sound of harsh voices and many booted feet. A woman, laughing—her words...lost to him. Cruel tone, but the words washed out in a haze of feelings that were foreign to Macsen. Bran's feelings? Trapped. Confined... then anger, a glimpse of a man, crowned, standing before a throne. Macsen focused on that image, Bran looking up past his chained hands at a human face.

Chains?

Chains.

"They put my beautiful Bran in *chains*?"

As if that was a key, the memories clicked into sequence in his mind. The girl, the staff, the woman. A man enthroned and the cage of black iron bars that came at his demand—the prodding of a hundred spears and the despair born of many nights spent all but hopeless. *Many nights.* Macsen's heart beat hard in his chest, and guilt flooded him. *How many nights?* How many nights since the morning he had left? Two days for him, but that was months for his Bran—

"I've been a fool. I should have woken him and killed them all then, I should never have waited—why did I wait? Just to make it easier to convince him?"

For only the second time in his long life, Macsen Cadoc felt the agony of regret. There was nothing he could do with that feeling until he had Bran in front of him again, until he could apologize and make right his wrong—but there was a greater wrong that had been done than Macsen's. Anger grew in him, cold fury like the brewing of a winter storm.

Macsen shoved himself out of his high seat with both hands and let out a roar that froze the sweating fervor of the dance.

"Milesians!"

Wrath like nothing he had ever felt before was pulsing in him.

Macsen leaped down from his throne, and with two great steps was at the center of his court. He called out to them all, loud enough to silence the pounding of the drums.

"*Sidhe*! You are my people, you are the court of the Red King! Do you miss the wild past, the days when the Wild Hunt was more than a whisper, more than a game to be played one night each year?"

Laughter and a murmur and a stumbling roar of voices saying "Yes, yes, we miss the past when we were free," answered him, and Macsen smiled.

"There are humans on the isle to the west that hunt us now, a whole people, dedicated to nothing but our destruction. They are Milesians, the same mortals who tricked Eire from Summer's people, who banished them to the hidden kingdom of their queen. How many of you once raced through the Irish night and vanished into the sacred barrows at dawn? How many of you miss rivers and forests where you lived through the immortal generations before men breathed? How many of you came here to me, to run in the Wild Hunt across Britain because the isle to the west was no longer yours?"

The murmur was growing, and Macsen gloried in it.

"We were there—we were there—we left those shores behind to join you—we were banned and barred from our own places—we miss our passage through our old lands—"

"Yes. I hear you. But the Milesians don't care for old gods or old powers. I've been among them—yes, I, your king. I've seen the evil there, the hatred they feed like a precious pearl, painting it with new luster at our cost. And they do this for prestige, for the sake of their human alliances!"

The words came poisoned from his tongue and crept from ear to ear. These were his dark companions, his Red Court—he knew them all, grim and gleaming, wild and wonderful. It was the most passionate *sidhe* of the ancient world who followed him, hunters and thieves, bloodthirsty shadows and the hollow voices of the night that feast on violence.

He had been ten years old when he had defeated the one who had been Red King before him. Only ten, in a kingdom of immortals, but they had accepted Macsen's succession because he was the strongest of them, because he was the best of them. Because he loved them for their submission and their brilliance, their deadly strengths. Macsen knew what they were expecting now, what they wanted—it had been his intention the moment he spoke to them.

They were riled now, blood-thirsting. The horses of the *dullahan* chafed at their shining bits of bone. Wide eyes of the *scáthanna beo*, his vampire kin, shone back at Macsen with a gleam like that of his own eyes, hungry and wanton. He looked one at a time at shifting, glittering fae with trembling wings, at pale shades and the ghosts of ancient warriors.

Macsen's grin grew wider. The host of the Hunt would grow tonight. He called out over the crowd and heard wild cries answer him from those already present.

"Call up the *sluagh* and the banshee, the *clurichaun* and the black dogs, the *fachen* and the fae tricksters!

For a thousand years we've waited in silence, but that time is over now. The Milesians broke the oath that bound the barrows of Eire, and an oath is not an oath unless both of those who have sworn it keep it."

His voice grew low and gathered danger, and the crowd around him hung on every word.

"Those of you who came from Summer to join me can return to your ancient places now, can run through your deep rooted barrows, but first find your kin, your long-lost companions. Tell them there is no barrier now between them and the world of men. The ways that were shut are open — the stolen prince was taken by an old and foolish foe."

Macsen cast his gaze around and saw straining eagerness. "The rest of you — the rest of you know the way!"

A great howl went up from the hounds of winter. The unearthly steeds of the *dullahan* screamed a scream to wake the dead, and the dead screamed with them. The restless horns of lost hunters went up, shaking the trees and the pale moonlight. Streaming shadow and shade, pale and ghostly and gleaming under the sky, the Red Court rose at its king's call and streamed out in howling immortal procession into the mortal night, each with their own purpose, their own darkness, their own promise of dreadful things.

Macsen stood still and let them flow out of the kingdom around him. He gorged his own black thoughts on the urges that broke and surged around him like a tide. Twin streams moved out across the winter whiteness, one moving sure and swift toward the barrow that had its opening in Anglesey, the other wavering across the limit of his vision, moving east toward the boundary of his Winter kingdom and Summer's land.

He kept to himself the real reason for his sudden passion, for this Hunt, for taking advantage of the promises that humans had broken twenty years before. He didn't care for Summer's freedom, would have kept his knowledge secret just to irritate the queen who had been his enemy, except that now he had a need for a great distraction. This would unleash the *sidhe* of the western isle, and his own Wild Hunt would roam without boundaries, a force for chaos if there ever was one.

It was Bran that was Macsen's concern, his Bran being kept in chains. Nothing would tame Macsen now except revenge.

He turned and strode quickly to his own chamber, stripped and dressed in red like the bloody light of sunset, just to make it obvious who he was. He took up the sword that had been laid on the bed beside the clothes, stared at it with a grim expression then hung it at his waist. It was the sword of the huntress, the one whose bones he had followed to Bran. It amused him to take her weapon, and Macsen thought it fitting that Bran should be avenged by a sword he had made.

Only after he was dressed and ready did Macsen stop to wonder how clothes and sword had come to be where he wanted them, when he needed them. When he turned, Talaith was in the doorway. Her eyes glowed with the promise of the Hunt, though her face was placid and amused as always.

"I trust that's all you need, my lord, and that I'll get to meet this Bran Fionnan you keep muttering about."

For the first time in Macsen's memory, Talaith grinned. Her teeth gleamed, silver needles in the dim light. Then she turned and vanished. He crossed to the window and saw her join in at the tail end of the court's procession, running out of the forest toward the barrow.

When the last of the stragglers had vanished, Macsen left his palace, empty now and echoing his footsteps back to him. Outside, he felt the rising of his kingdom and its powers broadcasting his intentions to any others who could feel the energies of the air. In return it brought him whispers of magic, reflections and promises, and he smiled.

Riders and darkling *sidhe* had already brought his stirring words to Summer's people. Just as he'd thought, more than just his court were riding in Hunt tonight. The banished *sidhe* of Eire, long outcast from the mortal lands they long had loved, were rising. His impromptu speech had woken the memory of human trespasses, and the rumor that the barrows were open had spread wide and fast. Summer's people were angry—very angry. They had been caged long enough, and now they knew the magic barrier of the oath was gone. If humans did not keep their word, why should the *sidhe*?

Macsen smiled to himself. Perhaps he had found Bran now for a reason. Perhaps it was time to take back the world that men dared to think was theirs alone.

"I'll give you the war you want, Milesians. War, and blood, and death."

He turned and followed the Wild Hunt into the mortal winter's night.

Chapter Six

Macsen left his kingdom behind him and passed over the white-flecked foam of the rolling waves of the Irish Sea. Leaping spray and the cry of night birds and selkie voices kept him company as he crossed the narrow water. The coast of Ireland loomed before him, a sudden gray shadow that grew on the surface of the sea like mist.

As if his presence was permission, Macsen set foot on the green shore and felt the great, straining host that had waited near the coast run across the land like a wave. The howl of the Hunt soothed the Red King only a little. In its wake, the lights of houses and farms, villages and towns, were lit one by one in terror and confusion. Those who saw what it was that had come for them were screaming, and those who didn't soon would be.

The woods grew haunted. From pools and streams and rivers came unearthly wails, the sounds of shuffling feet, the dripping tones of hollow laughter that curses human ears. Men and women caught unawares gave up their life's blood to the teeth of

Macsen's kin. The black hounds howled their death omens and the *dullahan* marked victims with buckets of blood. Murderers and mischief makers among the fae took lives and ruined orchards, blighted crops and fields, cursed cows and ewes to give sour milk, or none, or to die where they stood and join the haunted procession, eerily lowing.

Women sewing by the fire pricked their fingers and stared in horror at the things that crept out of the shadows to lap at the blood. He saw men on their way home from inns and taverns, men slow with drink who followed singing voices, beckoning fingers, and the lure of carnal, magic promises to early deaths.

That night, a hundred kingdoms of Britain and Ireland, Scotland and Wales began to pay the price for the distress that had been caused to Bran, and through him to Macsen. Farmers and princes of the Eastern isle knew the coming of the Wild Hunt when they heard it, even when it came on an unexpected night. Doors were locked, windows closed and barred, fires built high and old prayers said against the darkness—a few were lucky. The Hunt was wild but Macsen had ensured that its urgency was turned toward the Milesians. A little at a time the great host was moving westward.

Macsen crossed the land with terrible speed and watched his people and the Summer *sidhe* with pleasure, never so glad as now to see their terrible natures given full reign. He was called many times to join the fun, but he turned away from blood and mayhem, focused on his own purpose.

He stopped only when he came to the house at the top of the hill looking down at the river and the village, though he knew what he would find.

Emptiness.

No light, no presence — no Bran.

He stood before Bran's door and saw in his mind's eye the scene that had come to him in his dream. Bran's blood had been spilled here — here, he had been locked in chains. Men had come for him and taken him away. Men, and a little girl, and a woman. As he thought of the woman Macsen saw her face for the first time, clearly in his mind. It was Bran's view, a dream-image, her smile full of fear and cruelty, her eyes a hungry green.

The Red King's thoughts trembled between joy and rage, but the joy was only because the rage had proved his love to him.

He refused to live out the rest of eternity with this new need unsatisfied. The Milesians who had dared to steal his Bran — to steal him twice now, once from the mother who still mourned him and once from Macsen himself — they would die. Nothing could save them, not from the Hunt, and not from Macsen.

The night was sharp and cold around him, and Macsen breathed deeply of the winter air to soothe the angry fire within him. He should have returned the next night — no, he should never have left. He should have woken Bran and made him listen, seduced him in that moment, convinced him at any cost. Then he could have brought Bran with him into the dark.

"Even if I'd had to flee in the face of that woman...but I didn't know how much they'd dare. I didn't know, Bran Fionnan."

Macsen silenced his footsteps and cloaked the shriek of his presence, the dark energy that flowed out from him the way a shadow flows from the flickering of a candle. He would give the Milesians no warning, no chance, would neither retreat nor have mercy. He would slake his thirst on the guilty, and he recognized no innocents now.

One street, one alley at a time, Macsen prowled, seeking blood and information. He stopped outside the inn. It was full of voices — fearful voices speaking out against the king, angry voices speaking against the huntresses, sly voices speaking against anyone and anything that they could blame for the stirred up *sidhe* riding over their lands. One man, drunk and sitting beside a window, spoke louder and his words came clearly to Macsen's ears.

"I tell you, I've never seen anything like it, trees broken up all over, some monster swinging a chain and Seamus dead! The thing — the thing took his head right off — "

"Maybe the *sidhe* confused the islands, huh? Maybe they think this's Britain."

The first man dissolved into drunken hysterics, and that second voice spoke over it. "Oh hells, come on, Conall — "

A third, lower voice spoke over him. "Shut up, Aed. Don't tell me you didn't see th'shadows outside th'door. Don't tell me you're not staying here for th'same reason as us. You're a fool if you're not frightened. A thousand years we've been safe from th'*sidhe*, but tonight a darkness came and they came with it."

There was a moment of silence, and Macsen crept forward a few more steps until he could see the man who was speaking.

"Can't say I'm surprised. Mac Briuin's made a mess of much before this, and now th'king's got a *sidhe* locked up in his palace. Th'one that's called Rud — "

The second man, Aed, interrupted him. "So?"

"So maybe that wasn't th'best idea. Have you seen th'poor bastard? Th'king's got him in a cage next to his throne—"

"Not all of us get summoned to the king's feasts, Fergal."

Macsen heard the shiver of fear in Fergal's voice when he spoke again. "So? That's not th'point. I tell you, there's men been flayed alive in old stories for less than what th'king's done to that one."

Macsen stepped back from the inn then and turned toward the palace. The truth...that was it, then. And he wondered what it was that the man Fergal meant with his words. *"There's men been flayed alive in old stories for less..."*

A shiver of fury moved over Macsen's skin, cool and pure. He knew what he had to do. The Hunt had had enough time to serve as a distraction, it was time to let the Milesians know who had come to visit them. Macsen moved swiftly, sure now of his destination, and the power he had crushed into silence burst out like the blossoming of some deadly, sable flower.

Heavier than the night, sharp at the edges and weighted with blood, the presence of the Red King devoured the village and the palace in its shroud.

It took Macsen only a moment to make his way down the main road that led through the village. The shadows that spun and shaped themselves around the houses and shops flickered in the light of guttering torches and were drawn to him, unerring as the directional point of a compass.

He came to the palace and found it full of noises— the sounds of booted feet and jangling armor, weapons rubbing against each other and men calling to one another with voices that shuddered with fear. He heard women, too, but fewer and far between, and he smiled. The huntresses were missing, then. They would be out among the people, trying their best to beat back the onrushing tide of the Wild Hunt. It had been too long since they'd been threatened in their own land. Shadows of ancient days whose names the Milesians had forgotten, if they had ever known them, would haunt them until Macsen called them back, or they grew weary, or they ran out of men to slay.

Macsen smiled to himself and lifted his hands, pressed them to the palace's great oak gates. Once, twice, he knocked. His hand was heavy, the sound loud, impossibly loud. He waited, just long enough to feel the gazes of sentries fall on him, to hear cries of warning being shouted on the other side of the gate. Then he pressed his palms flat against the wood and pushed forward.

Strength of oak versus the strength of ages — the gate strained at its hinges for only an instant, then broke with a crash like thunder and a scream of splintering wood.

Shivering guards stood before him, blocking the way toward the king's hall with their bodies. They were warriors, perhaps tested in a hundred battles, but now they trembled though only one foe stood before them. Crowned and dressed in red, his whole being stained with shadow, Macsen smiled at the Milesian warriors and watched their lines waver and almost break from that alone. Despite himself he was impressed that they still stood firm, and he smiled wider and spoke in conversational tones.

"Hello, humans."

Before he had finished that second word they rushed at him, but they were only men. Even the best of the huntresses who *had* been so trained had failed to stop Macsen. The plight of the king's guards was hopeless, and one by one they fell beneath his strength, beneath his blade.

The sword Bran had forged for Noirine Muirenn flickered with gold and white fire under the moonlight.

* * * *

Bran was only half conscious when Macsen came for him. His perceptions were so dim that even the breaking of the gates and the commotion that accompanied it were nothing more than a dull wash of noise across his consciousness.

The last time he had really been awake, it had been night, and the moon had been dazzling — the moon of the third month, counting down the days to his sacrifice. Saoirse had come to him with water and roast meat and berries, and the memory made him aware of the emptiness in his gut, the dry tongue swollen in his mouth. It had been days since Bran had been fed, or given water, days since he had moved from where he lay, slumped over on the floor in the middle of his cage.

Days since Saoirse had been found by Dealla with her hands full of fruit, reaching through the bars of Bran's cage.

Bran's punishment was terrible enough, but he didn't know what they had done to the girl. Dealla had dragged Saoirse away, haranguing her, and Bran had heard screams that night and some nights since. He wondered if they'd killed her, or beaten her, or if they'd broken her.

Guilt surged through him. He should have told her to stop coming, to leave him alone —

"Not like...she would've listened. Stubborn thing..."

"Are you speaking, traitor? You still have breath enough to defy me? Shut your mouth!"

There were fear and anger both in Mac Briuin's voice when he spoke, and Bran turned his head a little and stared at him with dull eyes. A series of terrible screams rang loud enough from outside that Bran heard them clearly before they became silence. Bran started to laugh, a low, hollow sound, and the king got up on his feet and turned to shout at the cage, his voice shrill with fear.

"Enough—enough! You're only a beast—you're nothing—you'll die here, traitor!"

Bran's laughter ran down into silence, but he still smiled. He knew suddenly and completely what was happening outside. He knew who had come.

"Not going to die…you waited too long and now it's too late, Mac Briuin."

The man drew his sword, but he only had time for one step toward the cage before the doors to the hall were torn open. They hung crooked on their hinges, and the bar that had locked them shattered into toothpick-splinters.

Neither the sound nor the flying bits of wood stirred Bran, but Macsen's presence did. The Red King was real, no longer just a dream, and Bran's flickering vision focused on Macsen's eyes, their piercing violet brighter now than ever. He wore the same smile as the last time Bran had seen him, and Bran shook his head to see it. Slowly, one foot, one leg, one wavering movement at a time, he stood.

Bran licked cracked lips with a dry tongue. "You made me wait long enough, Macsen Cadoc."

Macsen came toward Bran with the moon reflected in his eyes, and Bran stepped forward, not back. He came to the very edge of the cage and pressed himself against the bars. Macsen reached out and shook them and the whole cage moved, screeching against the dais.

"I hardly waited at all, beautiful Bran. Don't you know that time is different for you than for me? This world moves faster. Mortal days are immortal hours. It was only the dream of you that told me you were in need — but when I knew it, I came. I should never have waited — I'm sorry."

"You did promise — "

"That I'd keep you forever? Yes. I'm everything you thought I was when you said it was wrong to want me, but I always keep my word. Now, to get you out of there."

Bran pointed at Mac Briuin. The man stood as if stunned, the point of his sword resting against the floor, his face and body slack with fear or surprise.

"He's the one with the key."

Macsen's face contorted and gained a savage expression that was both furious and soft. "Key? I don't need such a thing. Stand back, Bran Fionnan."

Macsen grasped one of the bars in each hand, shoulder width apart, then lifted the whole cage and tossed it aside. It had taken a dozen men to carry it in and settle it on the dais beside Mac Briuin's throne, and Bran could only stare at such a display of strength. The cage struck the tables on the floor of the hall as it went flying, and sent them tumbling across the dirt. The hall shuddered from the force with which the iron bars smashed against the wall.

Bran heard a whimper from Mac Briuin and grinned widely though his lip split and bled. What an honest sound! The whole nature of the man was in it, ignorant and fearful. In the face of death he abandoned pride and all the arrogant claims he had made in the months Bran had been caged beside him.

On Macsen's face Bran saw something feral, the expression of a beast that scents fear. For a moment Macsen appeared completely focused on Mac Briuin. Then he turned and the cool tingling of his fingers stroked Bran's cheek.

"Wait for me, Bran. Out of the way, there. This won't take long."

Macsen turned back to face Mac Briuin, and Bran limped to the limit of the circle of firelight cast by the flickering torches. His legs felt alternately like water and lead, and his vision was quick to blur if he turned his head too fast, but he wanted to watch. He wanted to see Mac Briuin die, wanted to see Macsen kill him. If he'd had the strength left Bran would have killed the man himself.

He heard the ring of steel and saw that the edge of Macsen's sword gleamed with gold. Macsen's voice tore at Mac Briuin like a whip, and the words brought a smile to Bran's face.

"Are you done playing games, little king? Are you done sending women after me, done with caging my Bran, done with devising new ways to earn death?"

My Bran, Macsen said, and for the first time in many days Bran felt a surge of warmth that didn't come from a half-waking dream. He was afraid he was still dreaming, that it wasn't really happening, but it was. *It was.*

You came for me, Macsen—

He didn't yet know why, nor did he care. That it was true was enough. That Macsen was *there* was enough. Bran watched Macsen circle the man who called himself king of the Milesians and saw that Mac Briuin was only a child in the body of a man, only a coward with a sword. Before Macsen, he appeared withered, powerless—so very *human*. The heavy, red-bearded features looked hollow now.

Macsen was a king, and beside him Mac Briuin was revealed as nothing but a petty tyrant caught mid-tantrum by a greater power.

Bran saw that clearly, just as clearly as he saw that the man would die.

* * * *

Macsen turned his full attention to the man standing before him and prodded Mac Briuin with words. He taunted the fear he could see in the bearded face.

"Cáelbad mac Briuin, do you know me as I know you?"

The man grimaced and Macsen saw his knuckles go white on the hilt of his sword.

"Yes, I know you. Vampire."

He said the word as if he meant it to be an insult, but Macsen only smiled.

"Tell me, little king—what was it you sought to accomplish, taking one who is mine for yourself?"

Macsen drew the sword he had brought with him and watched Mac Briuin's eyes widen as he recognized the blade. His mouth worked silently for a moment, until the dull glare of his eyes looked up past Macsen and stared toward Bran where he sat watching, his face impassive.

"Traitor—"

The word hissed past the man's lips and Macsen cut it to silence with a vicious backhand. Mac Briuin staggered and spat blood but kept his feet, and Macsen growled out words at him.

"No more words! Nothing, from you—you, who betrayed your pact with Summer's people, who stole one of the *sidhe*—you, who dare to call yourself a king!"

Mac Briuin showed his teeth and Macsen laughed.

"No, human, that's not how it's done."

He bared a mouthful of fangs and saw the man's sword waver, then lift just a little, so that it pointed at Macsen's heart.

"I'll fight you, vampire!"

He stepped forward, and Macsen reached out and caught his right wrist in a grip like a steel vise.

"No. No, your women try to fight me—your huntresses. All *you* can do is die."

Macsen let go of Mac Briuin's arm and shoved him back so that he stumbled across the open space before his throne. As soon as he had his footing, Mac Briuin rushed forward, on the attack, looking for some weakness, some opening.

Macsen could see the desperation on his face, thinning his lips, pulling the skin of his cheeks and forehead tight. The man's impetus was all fear, no real hope, no belief in his own strength despite the boastful words he'd spoken. Macsen tasted terror on the air between them, sharp and bitter. With ease he sidestepped each of Mac Briuin's heavy swings.

If the man's sword had connected, Macsen would have been wounded badly, but Mac Briuin was too slow, his strikes ungainly. He had none of the agility of the huntresses, and his perceptions were only the perceptions of a normal man. Whatever training those women used to hone their senses, Macsen could tell that this man hadn't been a part of it.

Macsen used that to his advantage. Silent, intent, his face settled in grim, dark lines, he taunted Mac Briuin with his ability to wound the man almost at will. The gold-edged blade flickered out again and again, slipping past all the man's attempts at guarding himself. In a matter of minutes Mac Briuin was bleeding from two dozen wounds, all of them shallow, narrow cuts. They were irritations, and the man knew it. Moment by moment, the man's fear was giving way to rage and it amused Macsen to watch it happening.

The next time Mac Briuin stepped forward, Macsen was ready. Instead of striking at the man's unprotected body he met the edge of Mac Briuin's blade with his own sword and stepped in, closing the distance between them as he pushed the man's arm off to the side. Like a grown man might hold off a child, expending no effort, Macsen held Mac Briuin still and bent to lick at a bleeding wound on the crest of his shoulder.

"You taste like greed, little king."

With a twist of his body, Macsen turned so that the man was in front of him. His right arm was outstretched into the air, his fingers tight upon the hilt of his sword, but the whole arm was pinned with irresistible strength.

Macsen held Mac Bruin's other arm behind his back, bent at a painful angle, wrist and elbow cracking with agony. Macsen looked over the man's shoulder toward the open space of the threshold with the remains of the door broken open across it. He could hear sounds from outside, and he knew the time for taunts was over. Immortal senses brought him the odors of blood and rage and deadly promise — a dozen women, each one a huntress.

Macsen tightened his grip on both the arms in his grasp and drank in the resultant cry of pain.

"Our time is up, Cáelbad mac Briuin. Do you hear them? The women who are coming for you, thinking they can save you? I can hear them, but you know as well as I do that they've come too late."

"Beast—*monster*—"

"Yes. The truth is no insult, little king."

The Red King met Bran's eyes as he tore open the side of Mac Briuin's throat with his teeth, then dropped the man to the ground.

Macsen wiped his sword on the hem of the dying man's tunic and crossed to where Bran was sitting, his eyes brighter now, his gaze fixed on Mac Briuin as he bled from the gaping wound at his throat and choked to death on the flood of gore. Macsen had no need to watch the man die. He was done with him, had spent so much time on him only because he had known it would be pleasing to Bran. He hadn't even been able to bring himself to drink the man. He had tasted like oil and iron and that wasn't pleasant at all.

Macsen reached out and touched Bran's cheek, and Bran turned to look up at him, grinning now.

"Not very nice, but now I see why they call you the Red King."

Macsen shrugged. "Was nice what you wanted, Bran Fionnan? *I* didn't think so."

He felt swelling beneath his fingertips, a bruise, a half-healed cut and a scar above that. Now that he had the time to look, really look, he saw that Bran was thin, too thin, and that the gold in him was all but faded, the blue of his eyes dim and restless. Bran's hair straggled down onto his shoulders and the grain-gold shock of blondness was wilder and darker than Macsen remembered it, though Bran's cheeks remained smooth.

Bran smiled, but it was as if the months of imprisonment had drained all the sun out of him. Not a hint was left. It was—wrong. The golden body Macsen so wanted to possess had grown pale. Beneath the skin stripped of its burnished hue, the marks of many cuts and bruises showed up dark against Bran's flesh.

"Bran, my Bran, missing me was bad for you."

"You've got an ego, haven't you? Do I need one of those before I'll fit in with the *sidhe*, Macsen Cadoc?"

"Ego? It's merely the truth, beautiful Bran."

"Flattery won't do much for you—"

"But that's only the truth, too. You're hard to please, aren't you?"

"I try."

Bran's grin was only a shadow of what it had been, but still it was there and Macsen was glad to see it. He wanted reassurance that he hadn't come too late. It was a reminder, he thought, that there were times when patience was the exact opposite of a virtue.

"If I'd waited one more day—"

Macsen didn't realize he'd spoken out loud until he felt Bran's hands on his face, heard him answering, his voice slow and almost laughing.

"If you'd waited one more day, then I'd be dead and you'd have less to worry about."

His voice was teasing, humor to make light, but their eyes locked together and Macsen shook his head. He leaned down and pressed his mouth fiercely against Bran's, tasted blood like fire where Bran's lips were broken and gave him blood in return, a spark of Macsen's own strength to soothe him.

"It's time for you to come with me, Bran Fionnan, away from this place and these people."

"There's one thing, first."

"Someone else you want to kill?"

"Someone else I want to *live*."

Macsen scowled, but Bran continued speaking anyway.

"There's a girl. Her name's Saoirse, and she kept me alive. She was his daughter..."

Bran's gaze flickered across the room to the body of Mac Briuin on the floor, and Macsen's scowl began to widen into a smirk.

"Macsen, if you can find her, if she's alive, take her away from here. Take her away so they don't kill her instead of me. Her sister Dealla's the one who's mad for blood, and I—" Bran paused. "They know she was helping me."

Macsen considered the words for a moment. *If she's alive* — would Mac Briuin have killed his own daughter for giving aid to Bran? He considered the black hatred he had seen in the man's eyes, the depth of fear there. Maybe. *Maybe.*

For Bran's sake he washed the dark thoughts from his face.

"You want me to steal her, Bran Fionnan? I'm surprised at you."

Bran grinned, but the expression was slower now. "Not steal her — save her."

"Save her...this fool's daughter."

Macsen watched Bran's eyes blink slowly, watched him shrug, his shoulders heavy with pain and weariness.

"I've got no claim on you, or your help—I know that, but—"

He closed his eyes and seemed to slump a little, and that alone made up Macsen's mind.

"But you came back. I was waiting—I kept on waiting even when I knew it was stupid, and you came back, so—help her, Macsen."

Macsen lifted Bran in his arms despite his protests, then turned and crossed the room to prod the dead body of Mac Briuin with a foot.

"I suppose it's only fair to steal a daughter from one who stole a son. I'll find her, or what happened to her. But it's time for you to go, Bran."

The sound of the footsteps he had been hearing outside had become loud and obvious, and women poured in through the open space of the broken door. Macsen stepped back with Bran in his arms and stood in the center of the room beside the body of their dead king.

One huntress stepped forward before the others and her gaze grew hard, taking in the body on the ground behind Macsen. She had no chance, the truth of that was in her eyes, but behind her, ten and twelve and twenty other women made their way into the room. They barred the way out with their presence, and a frustrated snarl crossed Macsen's face.

It was this that he had sought to avoid. One on one, he could destroy them. They were no match for him, any of them, even if some among them were a match for other *sidhe*. Even facing so many, in close quarters he was more deadly than any of these women could imagine. There were powers he possessed that he hadn't touched since the great heroes of the past had faded into the grass.

No...it was not their strength that concerned him, nor even the number of them, each one willing to die in the hope that one of her sisters might strike a deadly blow. It was that Bran was still in his arms, asleep or unconscious, worn with wounds and waiting — and that Bran had made a request. He must save that girl. *Saoirse*. What to do?

A thought occurred to him and he smiled.

Macsen whistled a piercing, unnatural note. The less experienced of the huntresses facing him bent at the waist and pressed their hands against their ears. A few dropped their weapons, and many began to look back and forth at each other, their expressions fearful as the earth itself began to shake. The hall rumbled and the great trunks of oak that had been used to build it vibrated against each other.

From beyond the barrier of worlds, Macsen's whistle summoned the *dullahan*. Long ago they had been one of the darkest servants of Summer's Queen, part of her inheritance from Summer's vanished King. For a thousand years they had been bound to obey Macsen, their promise and the reason he had allowed them to join his Hunt. It was a bargain he had found worthwhile, then, and now. No lock could bar the passage of the *dullahan*. No door, no boundary could stand in their way — that was why they had come to him, why they had found banishment untenable.

Before the *dullahan's* power the line of huntresses was no obstacle at all.

His horses came shrieking out of nothing and into reality, and a black wind and the odor of blood rushed with them as they passed over the threshold. The *dullahan* drove through the startled women on the box of a black carriage wrapped in shadow and screams.

The one who whipped the frothing horses was fleshless and bore a whip of gleaming vertebrae. He laughed at the fools who thought to surround his king, and his laugh was a shiver of terror. It had been an age and an age since the *dullahan* rode free in his ancient haunts and even these women, trained to fight supernatural foes, couldn't look death in the face. Most of them turned screaming and fled in a great press through the broken doors.

The *dullahan* came to a stop at Macsen's feet and spoke with a voice that was rust and hollow bones.

"My King, you summoned me?"

Macsen saw only one huntress left, she who had stood before the others. Her posture was straight and tall, her expression proud and hopeless and cruel. She was a thousand times more a queen, this one, than the dead man behind Macsen had been a king. He saw her staring at him, not distracted by the horrible figure that stood beside him, and smiled.

"You are *Dealla*. I owe you pain, woman, but it's my Bran who deserves your life. Be grateful he's in no condition to take it now."

"You—"

Her voice was thick with rage but Macsen turned away from her, unconcerned, and mounted the steps to the black carriage. Carefully, he placed Bran inside, then stepped back and nodded to the *dullahan*.

The horses sped away, and Macsen turned back and met Dealla's eyes.

"This Hunt is over for you."

In a blink, he was beside her, then behind her. His arm slashed outward, and he caught her in the back of the neck with a single sharp blow. Dealla dropped to the ground and sprawled there, unconscious. Macsen stared down at her for a long minute before he made his way out of the hall, leaving the woman to wake to a terrible headache and a worse mess. It was so tempting to kill her—but no. Her life was Bran's to take, to revenge himself with. He wouldn't interfere with that.

For now, he had other work.

"Where are you, Saoirse? Are you alive or dead?"

Macsen made his way through dark halls and chambers that were abandoned as he approached.

* * * *

Saoirse lay on her face, as she had for three days now. Her wrists were chafed and bloody, tied with rough cord to the head of her own bed. Her ankles were tied too, but she had managed to loosen those a little by pulling at them when they were bound. If she turned her head a little to the left she could see the window of her bedroom, but not out through it. The open shutter let cold air wash in over her—cold air, and chaotic noise. The cold had stung her back at first, the flesh raw from many beatings, but now she felt hardly anything. Her ears were tuned to the sounds of screams. She thought they belonged to guards.

She didn't like guards.

There had been a watcher with her, one of Dealla's huntresses set to ensure that she didn't get free or manage trouble even tied up as she was, but she was alone now. She had been alone since the noise began, listening to the world, all but numb to the suffering of her body.

When the door creaked open behind her she tried to turn and look at who had come into her room this time. Her watcher returning? Dealla, for another beating? Saoirse's back throbbed with painful anticipation.

Instead of the answer to her terrible expectations, she saw a beautiful stranger, and the stranger spoke her name.

"Saoirse Saorla. Are you Saoirse Saorla?"

"Yes, I'm—"

"Good. I was tired of looking but my Bran wanted you to be safe."

The voice that silenced her was quiet and cold, but she wasn't insulted. Saoirse sat in silence, absorbing the presence of the stranger, his few words already dense with promise. Saoirse felt cool fingers at her wrists, then her ankles, setting her free from the bonds that held her. There was pain, the sudden rush of blood to her hands and feet, but she'd felt worse in the last few days. Saoirse gritted her teeth and flexed her fingers, tried to sit up and found that there were still nerves in her back after all. Pain rushed over her, sucked a gasp through her teeth and held her still.

Calm, still, intense, the bright stranger-eyes watched her, and she lisped her most pressing question at the one hovering over her. She had to ask, even if she thought she already knew the answer.

"You said *my Bran* — are you...are you the Red King? Bran told me about the Red King — "

The stranger stood tall for a moment, regarded her in silence through violet eyes, then smiled, revealed gleaming sharp teeth. Saoirse let out a breath and looked up with wide eyes.

"You *are*. What...what are you going to do with me?"

"I'm going to steal you, little girl."

Saoirse stared at him for a moment, then pushed herself up slowly from the bed. Her feet were unsteady under her, and her fingers clutched at the bed frame, but her agreement was swift and certain.

"Yes, please!"

What was there for her here?

"Dress yourself quickly then, girl. I've wasted enough time here."

Stumbling, panting, shivering, Saoirse moved as fast as she could across the room, found a dress in her wardrobe and tugged it over her head. The movements opened whip weals on her back and shoulders. The fabric of the dress grew warm and sticky against her back as the flow of blood renewed, and she bit her lip to keep back tears when the coarse cloth rubbed against her torn skin. Her eyes darted here and there, moving from one thing to the next. She would never return here, she knew that without asking—was there anything she couldn't stand to leave behind?

Boots—a brooch her mother had given her—the hair band with the amber stone she loved so much—the cloak of dark fur that was her warmest winter wear. The weight of it pained her, but the heat it kept close to her skin was comforting. She spared a glance for the Red King, but couldn't read his face—still, best to be quick, best not to tempt fate. Was there anything else? Anything, anything else from the life she was leaving behind…

Her eyes lit on the tall staff in northwest corner of the room, dark wood and gleaming gold—the proof of her promise, the gift that had begun it all. Her gift from Bran Fionnan.

Staff in hand, she crossed the room and stood before the Red King, looked up at him then thought better of her manners and curtsied as well as she could.

"I have seen that weapon before, Saoirse Saorla. My Bran—he made that for you? *You* are a huntress, a little thing like you?"

Saoirse's eyes opened wide, then squeezed shut. Should she have left it behind? Did he not want her now, because she had been meant to be a huntress? A hundred excuses and pleas rose in an instant to her lips, then vanished when he bent and lifted her without even waiting for an answer.

"I will give you to someone I trust, little huntress. You will be brought to my hidden kingdom — you will be safe there, just like Bran Fionnan. Say goodbye to your mortal life."

She smiled at him.

"I already did that, when I thought I was going to die."

The Red King stared at her for a moment, his expression unreadable, and adjusted the staff that she carried so it lay lengthwise across her body. She gripped it tightly in both hands and listened to the swift-beating heart of the Red King through the chill of his chest pressed against her ear. The shadow of his presence wrapped around her just because she was close to him, and she smiled to think of what it was that was happening to her. How angry Dealla would be if she knew! To be stolen by the fae — of all the dreams that occasionally spoke to her childish heart, this was the most dangerous of all.

The Red King ran, out of the palace and soon out of the range of men and their voices. His footsteps were smooth over the roughest ground. The landscape flashed past like an embroidered tapestry in the moonlight — white hills and white forests, snow covered but for the black stems of the trees standing like solid shadows under the stars. Unerring, never turning, he made his way forward. Saoirse dozed then woke again, not sure if minutes or hours had passed, only to find that her savior was in the process of handing her to a stranger. It was a woman — no, a *sidhe*. Saoirse scrubbed sleep from her eyes with the back of her hands and stared at this new being.

The stranger was a tall female with wide, round eyes and teeth like needles that flashed in the moonlight when she smiled. Saoirse started away from that smile, the pointed teeth. She pressed against the Red King as if he were somehow less dangerous, clutched at the soft red silk of his tunic, but his hands were on her hands then, cold slender fingers prying her grip free.

"This is Talaith, Saoirse Saorla. She is one of mine, one I trust above all others—you, too, can trust her. Do you understand? You are safe with her. She will bring you to the Red Kingdom and show you many beautiful things."

"And Bran Fionnan?"

She clung to the Red King's tunic with both hands, stuck her out her lip stubbornly and stared up into his eyes, awaiting an answer.

"My Bran is safe too—did you think I'd let him be otherwise? But you've done well, helping him, and I forgive you. You will see him on the other side of the night."

Saoirse let go of him then, and allowed herself to be passed into the arms of the *sidhe* woman.

The round eyes stared down at her, curious and wide, and Saoirse saw the needle-teeth gleam in a smile that spread wide across Talaith's features. Talaith shared a long look with the Red King, and Saoirse gasped as the blood-stained linen of her dress peeled away from the wounds on her back and rubbed against them. Saoirse felt the sharp fingers dig into her shoulder and thigh, drawing her close to the *sidhe* woman's side.

Chapter Seven

Bran woke from blackness to blackness and couldn't tell where he was. Memory told him that wherever this was, Macsen had brought him. The trust that had brought him close to the Red King in the first place served him well now, reinforced by the closeness he had learned in dreams. Even as he had the thought, he felt Macsen's presence swelling near him, that wonderful paradox of warmth and winter cold.

A little at a time, Bran realized that he was in motion and for a while the swaying was soothing. His body ached, but less than it had since the day he had been taken from his house by Dealla. He tasted the tingling coolness of Macsen's blood in his mouth still. Was that what had revived him? He closed his eyes and relaxed into the sway of the speeding carriage.

Bran drifted in and out of sleep, heard sounds and voices and occasionally opened his eyes. Sometimes when his eyes were open he could see nothing, and sometimes he could see through a pane of shadow like Roman glass. What he saw confused him. Was he awake or dreaming? He had the sensation of time passing in long silences. Occasionally he saw the moon, and after a while Bran felt within himself the warmth and response that told him the sun was in the sky.

The sunlight washed over him like cool water through the shadow-glass. It invoked heat within him despite that, a comfortable burn like the burn of strong drink. He wondered at it but before long he was drowsing again. He woke only a little when Macsen came for him, and sank more deeply into dreams when he was lifted into the Red King's arms from the gleaming terror of the *dullahan's* carriage.

When he finally woke, and woke fully, Bran found himself alone in a dim, silent house of ancient construction. Macsen was nowhere in sight, nor did Bran feel his presence nearby.

He lay still for a while, running his fingers over the furs that covered him. The roof was thatched, and he watched dust motes and tiny pieces of falling hay as they floated down from the ceiling and drifted out of his sight. His body ached, but it wasn't bruises or sore muscles that moved Bran finally, it was thirst. He became aware of the sound of running water, and the sound of waves, and grew aware of the thickness of his tongue in his mouth, the dryness of his lips.

Bran sat up slowly, but there wasn't as much pain as he thought there should be — not that he was going to complain about it — and after a minute he pushed himself off the bed and crossed the room to the window.

On the table beneath it was an old-fashioned silver pitcher, ornate and full to the brim with clear water. Bran hurried to fill the cup beside it, and when he took his first sip he was sure nothing had ever tasted so good. He drained the rest in one long draft, sucked in a deep breath, and panted a bit. He refilled it and drank more slowly, but when he put it down his stomach gurgled unhappily.

With his thirst quenched, Bran was starving. He cast his gaze around and spotted a hearth warm with embers, the bed he had been laying in, piled high with furs...and another low table, pushed against the wall on the other side of the hearth.

A bowl on it was piled high with fruits in colors that seemed too bright to be real. Another was overflowing with small loaves, and a small dish held creamy yellow butter. Bran ripped one of the loaves in half and slathered the open end, tore at it with his teeth then forced himself to chew slowly. It was the best bread he'd ever had, aromatic with herbs and some faint floral odor.

When he went to take another bite and found that he'd eaten the loaf, Bran took a handful of berries and an apple and another of the loaves of bread. He juggled the food in his hands and opened the door with his shoulder. It opened with a creak, and Bran looked around while he ate. The fruits were tart and sweet, bursting with juices, but the riot on his tongue wasn't matched by the view.

The land was obscured by a gray haze of mist, and colors seemed dull. Munching the loaf, tossing his apple from hand to hand, Bran walked in the direction of the sound of water. He didn't have to go far, a shallow stream rushed over the land not forty paces from the little house. Bran bathed in the cold brook, pleased to get the blood and dirt of his imprisonment off his skin despite the chill.

He listened to the sea while he shivered and shook water out of his hair, but he couldn't see it behind the wall of obscuring mist, a boiling curtain that billowed and curled across the landscape. It wasn't like any weather of the world that he had ever seen before.

"Must be magic. I wonder if *he* did it."

There was only one *he*.

Alone with his thoughts, alone with his memories, but most of all *alone*, Bran Fionnan spent several days doing nothing but eating and sleeping, thinking and dreaming. The pains he had suffered seemed to recede into the distance of his mind as his body healed. He wandered the empty space bound by mist, a great circle beyond which fog prevented his passage. This place...wherever it was, it couldn't be the Red Kingdom.

It was calm and cool, but there was no *difference* between it and the place he had spent so many years. *Sidhe* lived in the Red Kingdom, so if this was *there*...where were they, and where was the Red King?

"Macsen Cadoc, if you're out there...if you're out there, what are you waiting for? Where have you brought me? What am I supposed to be doing?"

The mist deadened the sound of Bran's voice, then parted in front of him. It rolled back like heavy clouds from between a pair of leafless trees. Macsen's voice came first, then his solitary figure walked up toward Bran between curling banks of mist that parted before him.

"I was waiting for you, Bran Fionnan. I can do nothing without your permission, can't take you home with me unless you say *yes*."

The Red King gleamed with immortal promise in the half-light of that place, but Bran was just glad to see him. He was almost—*almost*—startled by how much, but he let the warmth settle within him without fighting it.

"What is this place?"

Macsen laughed. "This is *between*, the isle that stands between the world of men and our world."

"Our world—"

"Yes, ours. Yours as well as mine. This is only Anglesey, the island that hides the entrance to my dark kingdom—the isle men call *Ynys Dywyll* and *Ynys y Cedairn*. The Dark Isle, the Isle of the Brave—the strong come here, hunting danger, and become my prey."

Bran grinned and stretched a little. "Your prey, huh? Is that what's happened to me?"

Macsen grinned, and moved close to him. "Of course."

Bran shook his head and laughed. "Did you—did you find the girl? Saoirse?"

The question escaped in a rush. Bran wasn't sure he wanted to hear the answer until Macsen smirked and reached out to touch his face, pushed the too-long wildness of his hair back out of his eyes.

"You doubt me! I'm wounded. Yes, I found her, and you were right to be worried for her. Someone had beaten her bloody, more than once, I think—it was lucky for her that you thought to ask me for her life."

Bran shook his head. "No, it would've been luckier for her if she'd never met me."

Macsen shrugged. "She doesn't think so."

Bran looked up, startled. "You—spoke to her?"

"When I found her. I gave her to someone I trust and now she's home—our home, Bran. She's waiting. She wants to see you."

Amusement played on Bran's face. "Someone you trust. You mean Talaith."

Macsen's eyes went wide with surprise and he smiled. "So, you've been dreaming, too."

Bran blinked. "Too?"

"I told you before—it was the dreams that told me who you were when I found you."

"That's—good?"

Macsen took the last step that separated them and nodded, leaned forward and brushed his mouth against Bran's lips. The warmth that Bran had been feeling began to blossom. He reached out and wrapped his arms around Macsen, pressed his body as close as he could get. Macsen kissed him again, more roughly.

"Very good, Bran Fionnan."

* * * *

Macsen ran his thumb down the line of Bran's throat, watched Bran shiver and bent to nip at the soft, trembling flesh. Blood welled up to the surface and Macsen lapped at it, savoring power.

"Even if it doesn't burn me, it's still strong—the sunlight bottled in your blood."

He spoke in the barest whisper, licked his lips of the taste of it again and again. Bran's hands wandered across Macsen's shoulders and sought impatiently for skin, sensation, closeness. Macsen laughed and tumbled Bran into the damp grass, caught his arms and pulled them up over his head. He held Bran still and delighted in the sight before him. The blue had grown dark in Bran's eyes again, a blue as rich as cream, and the gold that flowed beneath his skin was bright again. Bran struggled, trying to get closer. Macsen took pleasure in denying him, in teasing him.

"Be still."

"I don't want to be still, I want *you*."

"You say that so easily—"

"It's just the truth. I waited long enough."

Macsen bent and kissed him, bit Bran's lips and licked them, touched Bran's tongue with his tongue and felt urgency return to the movement of Bran's body beneath him. He took his time stripping Bran of his tunic, enjoyed the feeling of warmth under his hands, the shivers his touch produced in his lover — the way Bran rocked his hips between Macsen's thighs.

Macsen's fingers trailed over Bran's arms, his shoulders, traced his collarbone then followed his sternum down, down... Bran almost laughed. Was he ticklish? Macsen made a note to find out — but later. Later...

For now he used his fingers, his mouth, his tongue to trace lines of sensation across Bran's skin. He felt the swift heat of Bran's erection rise between them, leaned forward and trapped Bran's straining cock between their bodies. Delicate, almost gentle, Macsen pulled at Bran's nipples and watched new expressions of need and desire play across his face. Bran was obviously impatient, almost irritated, and Macsen kissed him deeply and took his time drawing his hands up the long lines of Bran's body.

"You won't always be so lucky as to be spoiled by me, Bran Fionnan. Enjoy it while it lasts."

Tongue, and teeth, and Bran's fingers dug into Macsen's back, scraped over his shoulders and tried in vain to pull Macsen against him, inside him. Macsen hovered, and laughed and denied. Bran moaned, unsatisfied.

Macsen teased him unmercifully. Macsen wanted to touch everything, taste everything — wanted to reassure himself in the most primal way that Bran was *here* and *his* and going nowhere. His tongue, his lips, the nipping of his teeth touched everywhere but the one place he knew Bran wanted it most. Macsen felt Bran shifting under him, his hips rocking, easing the rigid heat of his erection against Macsen's body. Macsen smiled and reached between them and stroked with loose, slow fingers around Bran's cock.

"Oh yes—"

Macsen licked the moan from Bran's lips, then leaned back and moved himself down Bran's legs so that he straddled him just above his knees. With an easy, swift motion Macsen stripped off his own tunic and tossed it on the ground. He watched Bran's eyes watching him, stroked the underside of his own erection with a single smooth finger and contemplated what would be best—what he should do next—

"You want pleasure, Bran?"

"Bastard—look at me, what do you think!"

Macsen did look, dragged his eyes over every inch of naked skin, focused on brown nipples tightened into sensitive pebbles, on the twitching of Bran's fingers, the compulsive way his tongue wet his lips.

"Beautiful, Bran. If you want pleasure then give yourself pleasure—but slowly."

Bran stared as if confused, then flushed dark in a pleasing way.

"Touch—myself?"

Macsen licked his lips. "*Yes*."

Arousal burned in him—was this innocence? No...but Bran must know he would be vulnerable, exposed—that was everything Macsen wanted. Macsen reached down and grasped the rigid length of his own erection again, enjoyed the sensation coupled with a gorgeous view. At first hesitant, it only took a few moments for Bran to become absorbed in his own pleasure, and Macsen matched the strokes of Bran's hand with his own movement, watched the dark flush of embarrassment fade from beneath Bran's skin and return, darker, no longer embarrassment but lust. Macsen's eyes were drawn again and again to the hard thickness of Bran's erection, to the thin pearls of liquid that beaded at the head of his cock then slipped down the straining shaft beneath Bran's fingers —

And all the while Bran was begging for more attention than the slow stroking Macsen allowed. When Bran tried to speed up the motion, Macsen reached out and held him back, savored the groan of frustration, of pleasure, of want as it slipped out of Bran's throat.

"You have never teased yourself this way?"

Macsen heard his own voice darken, rough now — it was almost as hard to restrain himself as it was to hold back Bran. Mutely, his eyes almost closed, Bran shook his head. Time passed, and Macsen waited until Bran's breaths were almost cries, sharp on the inhale, husky exhale — exquisite, the torture that was visible on his face every time Macsen reached out his own hand to take Bran's away.

Bran's cock throbbed red and rigid in his hand, and Macsen saw the moment when Bran couldn't take it anymore. The strokes of his hand grew faster, his breath heavier, deeper. His pupils dilated, and the muscles of his legs quivered beneath Macsen's thighs with pleasured tension.

"Enough, Bran —"

He reached out and pulled Bran's hands away from himself, but this time Bran struggled, panting, teased to distraction. He pressed with all his strength against the settled weight of Macsen's body, but Macsen had more leverage, the better position, greater strength.

"Macsen — you — *please if you make me stop* — if you make me stop — "

Eyes half-lidded, Macsen stared down at Bran and licked his lips as if those begging words had seasoned the air between them. Only when Macsen couldn't resist any more himself did he give in to Bran's incoherent pleading. He let go of Bran's hands and leaned down over his body, reached out his tongue to taste Bran's straining arousal.

Bran jerked beneath him at the first touch of heat and rough wetness. The muscles in his thighs trembled again and again, begging as much as his voice, but Macsen only continued to lick, to lap with slow, long movements of his tongue.

Holding Bran beneath him, hearing his sounds, tasting his skin, fulfilled some unsatisfied craving of which Macsen hadn't even been aware. A duller, quieter thirst than the thirst for blood was being sated, a little at a time. A thought drifted across Macsen's mind then, and he was amused by it not because it was true but because the thought of it being anything but true was...impossible.

This one is mine. Mine forever.

How could he ever grow tired of someone so sublime? Bran was all he had ever wanted and the answer to all his needs—stubborn enough to satisfy, brilliant enough to intoxicate and leave him without regret.

"Perfect...absolutely perfect."

He closed his mouth around Bran's cock and felt his own arousal climb. Macsen drew his tongue across the sensitive spots below the head, savored the texture of hot silk in his mouth. It didn't take long before Bran bucked beneath him and let out a sharp, broken cry. Macsen tasted some of the same heat in Bran's pleasure that was in Bran's blood, and more than heat. Salt, and musk—*Bran.*

Bran's cry was wordless, and he dug his nails into Macsen's back, Macsen's shoulders. The sting slid down Macsen's spine and settled along the sensitive nerves in his groin, pulsing for want of attention.

Macsen pulled back, licking his lips, and Bran shuddered and groaned just like Macsen wanted.

He leaned close and pressed his lips to Bran's throat, his chest, his shoulder.

"Now, do you still want what you were asking for, beautiful Bran?"

Macsen gathered slickness on two fingers and pushed them deep into Bran's body. Bran clenched his fists in the grass and pushed himself up enough that he could press his mouth to Macsen's mouth.

"*Yes*—damn you—yes—"

He dropped back onto the grass and Macsen lifted his legs and parted them, pulled Bran up so the curve of his back was sharp and high and pressed deep and slow and fully into Bran's body. *Heat.* Velvet. Macsen drew in a deep breath and thrust slowly, felt the intensity of the feeling crawling up the back of his calves, driving against the nerves in his spine, spreading from his cock like fire.

"Bran—"

And again.

"*Bran.*"

Bran groaned in time with Macsen's thrusts, and Macsen's gaze focused on Bran's erection as it thickened again, grew hard and drew up tight against Bran's belly. Bran took it in his hand, stroked roughly, his eyes locked on the length of Macsen's cock as it pushed into him. Macsen ran his hands up Bran's legs, tightened his grasp and bent forward, thrust faster, more sharply.

His nails left red welts on Bran's hips. He bit the soft flesh of Bran's thigh, sucked heat into his mouth and felt the pounding of Bran's heartbeat surge through him, felt the tightness inside Bran grow tighter, squeezing. A river of sounds and words jumbled together tumbled out of Bran's mouth. Macsen heard his own name, and *please*, and *deeper, I want — you deeper*.

It was enough.

It was too much.

Macsen drove himself as far into Bran's body as he could go, saw wet threads of white lust spurt hot and viscid across Bran's belly. The cry that accompanied that sight rolled through Macsen. Ecstasy stunned him. The velvet vise of Bran's body gripped him hard, and Macsen let out one great, sudden breath in a deep groan. Spasms of pleasure convulsed him, and he rocked his hips against Bran's buttocks, insensible to anything but the feeling.

A little at a time, Macsen's hands relaxed their fervent grip on Bran's legs. He pulled away, and heard Bran's moan of protest when his body was empty with a pleasure that almost pushed him forward to begin it all again — but no. Macsen drew his hands over Bran's skin, slow, calming now, closeness without the intensity of lust. Bran's flesh felt hot against his cool fingers as his own nature stripped him of the heat that came from Bran's blood.

Bran relaxed, the tension in his muscles softening, fading under Macsen's touch and vanishing into sleep. Macsen lay still beside him for a long while, letting his fingers trace errant patterns on Bran's back, enjoying the warmth of the body pressed against him. He contemplated his feelings, his desires, how each time he was close to Bran he wanted less to let him go. The bond between them had been meant to build trust between allies, to plant the seeds of friendship, to prevent betrayal—it had not been meant for love.

That didn't change the fact that in Bran, Macsen had found a consort who pleased him in all the ways there were to be pleased. A lover who could never hurt or betray him, a lover he could never hurt or betray.

Macsen wanted the future he could imagine with Bran at his side. The long years that had lain empty before him seemed suddenly full...as long as he could keep Bran beside him. The green hills of the western isle were open to the *sidhe again*. Summer's Queen would know by now that the Milesians had broken the pact, and that he, the Red King, had found the missing prince. She would want to see him—soon. Perhaps he had acted too rashly, rousing the Hunt, sending out those messages...

"But I was angry. I am *still* angry—but you are more important, Bran."

Macsen stared down at Bran and felt the burning of his fury, embers just waiting for a breath to spark them into life again. He reminded himself that he had killed the Milesian king. Part of the price for the pain those people had caused Bran had been paid, and Macsen had given Bran time alone, time to heal, time to come to terms with his new freedom. Macsen had been rewarded for his wait. Bran had called for him...Bran wanted him. There was only one other thing Macsen needed now.

"Bran Fionnan..."

He reached down and brushed blond hair away from Bran's eyes, shook his shoulder gently.

"Bran, do you hear me? Come home with me, come back where you belong."

"Mmm...home? I want...I want to go home but—" Once, twice, Bran blinked, then smiled. "Macsen. You better not go anywhere..." He paused, yawned. "Anywhere without me."

Then he closed his eyes again and pressed his body back against Macsen. Macsen looped his arm around Bran's waist, pleased with that answer. It was the permission he had wanted all along. Anglesey was his place as much as any place in this world could be his, and while he sustained the mists it was safe from anyone. Despite that it was still a part of the mortal world. It wasn't a final destination, just an in-between point, and now that he had Bran's agreement there was nothing to keep him on this side of reality.

"I was only here for you...and you are already mine."

Bran didn't move, and Macsen disentangled himself gently. He stood and dressed in his discarded clothes, then turned back to Bran sleeping on the grass. Macsen bent and lifted him and he stayed limp in Macsen's grasp, legs dangling, head against Macsen's shoulder. He was dead weight, dense and warm.

"Sleep, Bran Fionnan. Sleep in the light you carry, the light you bring."

Macsen brought his mouth close to Bran's cheek and let the weight of his whisper carry it like mist to Bran's ears, a suggestion and a sorcery. From deep sleep Bran sank deeper, and Macsen felt the utter relaxation of the body in his arms.

He no longer feared that Bran would leave him—not after Macsen had saved him, not after those words. *Better not go anywhere without me.*

It was just tradition to steal a sleeper and let them wake on the other side.

* * * *

Saoirse wandered a trio of beautiful rooms, alone. They were hers now—Talaith had said so when she put her in them. The *sidhe* woman had spoken only to tell Saoirse that the rooms were hers, and not to leave them without company. There was a room with a bed, and a room with a short table and many cushions and a room that held a steaming river. It flowed through a tub with high sides, and Saoirse bounced on her toes and stripped out of her stained, torn dress as fast as she could.

The heat was pleasant after the cold of the Red Kingdom, and it was nice to be able to wash the blood and grime from her skin despite the hot sting of the water on her back. After a time her wounds ceased to pain her except when she stretched her arms too far, or bent too suddenly. It was only when her fingers were wrinkled as raisins that Saoirse stopped splashing and got out of the bath.

In the bedroom, she found a wardrobe full of beautiful silks, gowns, robes and dresses. She touched the glittering fabrics with her fingertips, then closed the door and went to grab one of the furs from the bed. It was warm and soft, and she couldn't bear to think of staining any of those beautiful clothes with blood.

Drowsy, but unwilling to sleep sat by the window and peered out at the gleaming temptation of the new world below her. If she hadn't been so tired, and the littlest bit afraid, it would have been hard to obey the restriction Talaith had placed on her. As it was, her resolve was sorely tested when a sudden commotion drew her attention to the edge of the dancers, where the dark forest opened into the clearing that held the great tree of the Red King's palace. She looked down and saw the Red King himself, an unmistakable figure striding across the court with Bran Fionnan naked in his arms. Bran looked much better than he had the last time Saoirse had seen him, through the double cage of her sister's arms and the iron bars that had held him back. She went to the door that she knew led out into the rest of the palace, and stood there for a moment debating the possible consequences of breaking the rules in this strange place full of unknown dangers. She wanted to see Bran, wanted to talk to him and share all the strangeness she'd discovered so far.

Even as she made up her mind to open the door and go find Bran, it was opened from the other side.

She jumped back, intent on looking like she had been doing anything else, but Talaith only smiled at her and crossed the room to sit by the window.

"You saw the Red King return, little girl?"

Saoirse nodded eagerly, and peered over the windowsill, but Macsen and Bran had vanished from her view.

"The one the king carries — that is Bran Fionnan?"

Again, Saoirse nodded. She turned away from the spectacle of the dance beneath the window and sat up beside Talaith, kicking her feet against the wall.

"Talaith, will I be able to see them soon? I want to make sure Bran's all right, and I should thank the Red King —"

"I think the Red King will be most pleased you with you if you give him a little time to introduce his lover to the world he wants to share."

"I suppose..."

She was silent for a moment, then turned her eyes back toward Talaith.

"How long do you think it will take?"

Talaith sighed. "It will take as long as it takes, girl." She stood. "Come, let's find something to distract you for a while. You have wounds that need healing, and then we shall find something lovely to dress you in— all that red hair you have, you look like the Lady Morgan…"

Saoirse took the hand that Talaith held out for her and submitted to being pulled out into the hall.

* * * *

Macsen made his way across the land, down into the shadowed hollows, down to the barrow which was the entrance to his kingdom. He sped through long halls that grew distorted as he passed through them. Earthen walls paraded before him endless and dim— or were they wide open spaces, a forest of darkness greener than any wood that lived outside the barrow? Macsen turned left, always left, until he came to a place where there were no walls and the forest was reality. He breathed deeply of the cold air of his own realm. Always cold, always winter, here where no dawn had ever disrupted the rolling path of the moon…his own place.

Macsen stood still for only a moment, then darted forward across a meadow of silver-bladed grasses beneath white snow. A curving log, all that remained of some deciduous giant, bridged the deep river that flowed dark across snowy meadows and under the shade of the wood. Macsen crossed it with perfect balance, one eye on the way before him and the other on Bran's face. Macsen leaped off the end of the log when he reached the farther bank, then turned toward the forest that loomed before him. *Almost home.*

The living energies of his own place surrounded him. Wild magic, frozen promises, the speaking of the land and the whispers of those who lived in it all reached out for him, wrapped around him and comforted him even as those things were comforted by his return.

He passed them by without pausing, gathering threads of magic and meaning as he went.

His palace was the heart of the forest.

An improbable orchard steamed green and strange among winter gardens and courtyards full of ice, and Macsen passed through it and stopped amid greenery that curved around the base of a single tree much greater than all the others.

Open doors stood between curving roots at the base of that tree, his palace and those roots served as guide for walls manufactured with strange powers. The empty spaces had been filled with mist that gleamed like smoked glass, almost solid, patterned with delicate whorls.

Some among his people spoke in greeting as Macsen passed, but more stares followed him than voices spoke. They drew back from the wave of his presence, then crowded close behind him again once he had passed.

Macsen didn't care for their interest—he was intent only on Bran. He answered no one, and met no eyes. The spell of sleep would only last so long, and he didn't want to it to wear off in the middle of his court. There were marvels here like nothing Bran had ever seen, and terrors enough to chill and break him, but there would be time enough for all those things later.

Overwhelming Bran with all of it at once wasn't something he wanted to do. If Macsen was honest with himself he was hoping for Bran to grow used to the idea of life with him before the rest of the Red Court became a distraction — before Summer's Queen sent her messengers with questions and began to demand time with her son.

He reminded himself that he had rescued Bran from terrible danger — but it had been his fault Bran had been in such danger in the first place. Macsen grit his teeth and pushed down his feelings of guilt as he climbed the spiral stair that led up to his own rooms. In his bedchamber, with the doors shut, the murmur of outside noises faded to a bare whisper and Macsen let out a long sigh.

"I have to put my trust in you, Bran Fionnan. I have to believe that you meant what you said."

Better not go anywhere without me.

Macsen laid Bran on his bed and tucked him under soft, dark furs. Then he vanished behind a door in the western corner of the room that opened and closed on the sound of running water.

Chapter Eight

Water ran down into Bran's dreams until he found himself coasting on its current. He woke suddenly, but the sound of water was still with him, and when he opened his eyes he thought he was still dreaming. Above him, dark wood rose higher than his eye could follow. He couldn't see a ceiling, and the grain of the wood was...odd.

"Am I inside a tree?"

Bran yawned and he cast his gaze around a bit more. The room around him was familiar, but it wasn't until he pushed himself up on his hands and sank halfway to his elbows in rich fur that he saw that the room around him was the same one he had seen in his dreams of Macsen. He heard the sound of water coming faintly from behind a door in one corner and knew it was that sound which had woken him.

In the same moment Bran remembered in one great rush what had happened before he'd fallen asleep.

"I called for Macsen—"

Memory pulsed hot in him. Bran felt his body respond and tried to ignore his desire. There were more important things to worry about—like how this wasn't the little house he'd been staying in.

If this was Macsen's chamber, the bedroom he knew from his dreams, then Bran knew where he'd been brought. A wave of excitement rushed through him and sped his pulse, his breathing, his thoughts. A *sidhe* kingdom...the home of the Red Court.

For the second time in his life, Bran had been stolen. The first time he had barely known what was happening, and of that long ago theft he remembered only darkness and pain. This second time, he had been stolen from lies and brought to the truth. From death he had been returned to the promise of immortal life.

Warmth flushed through him like a hot wind. Bran grinned and couldn't restrain himself any longer. He flung his legs over the edge of the bed and pushed himself to his feet, went to the window of the Red King's chamber and looked out. His eyes darted from one point to another as his attention was drawn outward across a winter landscape of endless mist and mystery.

A hollow place inside him he had never recognized or understood was racing to be filled now, reaching out to the land for a lifetime's worth of warmth and reassurance. There was little warmth here, only the waiting sense of winter, but the reassurance—he had plenty of that. It was in the air, something he could taste, something with a fragrance that reminded him of copper and Macsen.

Bran leaned forward, his eyes seeking toward the horizon, and stared out at the winter landscape until a voice startled him.

"Are you planning to jump out the window, Bran Fionnan?"

Macsen's voice was unexpected, and Bran stumbled backward two full steps then turned to meet the indigo glow of Macsen's gaze with fierce temper.

"Don't be stupid. Why would I do something like that when I'm here?" Bran looked back out the window and drew in a deep breath. "Finally here — this is faerie, isn't it?"

Macsen nodded. "Yes, that's so. But what you see is only one piece of a greater realm. This is the Red Kingdom, my kingdom. What mortals call *faerie* is the whole of the hidden kingdoms, the other world that exists at the borders of reality, the secret lands where what is immortal lives out of mortal sight."

Bran blinked thoughtfully. "How many kingdoms like this are there? How many hidden places?"

"Eight kingdoms, tied to the mortal world — seven, besides mine. I rule the Red Kingdom, the dark half of winter."

"And I'm — Summer's son?"

"Yes...the son of Summer's Queen. Once, your mother was the Sapphire Queen, and she ruled only the sunlit half of Summer. When the Summer King's foolishness became known, she...*inherited* the rule of Summer's darkness, too."

"Who are the others?"

Macsen listed them off on his fingers. "The White Queen, the Amaranth Empress, the Black King and the Green King."

"But...I thought you said there were eight kingdoms. With you and my mother, that only makes six."

"The Green King rules the whole of spring. Really it should be known as one kingdom, but he counts it as two, just like your mother's Summer. The Jade Prince and the Lady of the Leaves do the Green King's work for him. Spends too much time in the mortal world, I hear — but we've only ever met once."

"Only once?"

Bran was curious, but Macsen only smiled and nodded.

"Yes. I don't often travel out of my own kingdom, unless it is to Hunt, and not many visit this winter court where the sun is forever dark...except now in you."

"In — me?"

Faster than his eye could track, faster than Bran had ever believed moving was possible, Macsen was beside him, the grip of his hands cold and strong and compelling on Bran's shoulders. The fingers of Macsen's left hand sent a shiver racing down Bran's spine from where they touched the back of his neck. Macsen leaned forward, his breath a ghost that trembled in the curve of Bran's ear.

"Don't you know what it means that you're the son of Summer's Queen? The son of a Summer Queen who rules two kingdoms, and only one by right?"

Bran met Macsen's gaze. "*No*. I was a child when I was stolen, or did you forget? All I know is what they knew, and they knew power like mine could kill your kind when they couldn't." He stared down at his own hands. "They needed a weapon they could control, but they still didn't trust me, they never trusted me — that's why — "

Bran stopped and shook his head. He didn't want to think about it. He didn't want to remember the days that had piled on him, one after another, while he lay with his arm over his eyes trying to block out the bars that caged him.

Macsen had meant to tell Bran about the things that bound them together. He wanted to answer all of

Bran's questions, wanted to make Bran happy so that he would agree to stay and not be tempted away to his mother's kingdom. They were lovers, but he wanted a deeper bond between them than the bond of flesh. He wanted an admission of emotion from Bran to match his own love.

Macsen wanted Bran to tell him that the trust he felt was real. He wanted Bran to tell him that he would stay.

But Bran's words thwarted his purpose and reawakened Macsen's desire for revenge. Low-voiced words escaped him.

"I won't forgive them and I won't forget, Bran Fionnan. Not as long as you are mine, not ever."

Bran glowed with fierceness to mirror Macsen's thoughts. His skin, his eyes, even his hair shone golden. He stood out in the darkness of Macsen's bedroom like a gilded idol, too gorgeous to resist — but Macsen didn't want to resist.

"Bran, beautiful Bran." In a whirl of movement Macsen took Bran and pressed him against the furs of his bed. "Say you love me, and that you will stay."

The words came out hot against Bran's skin, and Macsen felt him shiver. Bran's voice escaped him heavy and raw.

"Why would I say *I love you*, why would I — do that?"

The breathless tone of Bran's voice told Macsen everything he needed to know, but those words weren't what he wanted to hear. His response was immediate.

"Because I love you, Bran Fionnan. Because I want you here with me forever, I want you to feel what it is I feel for you."

Bran's struggles stopped. He lay pinned beneath Macsen's weight, and Macsen felt Bran's heart pounding through his ribs like a beast that wanted to be free. He knew what he had to say then.

"You'll be my consort, Bran Fionnan. Though you're the son of Summer's Queen, you'll be the prince of my Winter court."

Love.

"You'll stand beside me, you'll dance with me, you'll be the only one I touch until the end of time."

Desperation.

"Tell me you love me, Bran Fionnan!"

Madness.

For the first time in his long life Macsen Cadoc felt a twinge of fear. He knew what he felt—knew it, couldn't deny it, wouldn't even try. Neither doubt nor denial was in his nature, but Bran...Bran was as much *sidhe* as Macsen was, but he had been raised by humans.

What if he said *no*?

* * * *

Bran had a word now for what it was that Macsen felt for him, what it was that he felt in response. It told him why Macsen had chosen him to slake his lust, why Macsen had come back to save him and why he wanted Bran to stay with him forever.

Love.

Bran had no experience with it, had only the dim golden memories of a happiness from which he had been stolen and the softness of the woman who had raised him and died. What did he feel for Macsen? Not that warmth, but something like it and something more.

A feeling, but not just a feeling.

A thing to which trust and desire had given birth. An inexplicable name for an inexplicable thing.

"Love…"

The word slipped from Bran's lips but it was barely a whisper. He felt Macsen's hands on his skin and Macsen's teeth on his throat. A murmur of words carried to Bran's ears on a whisper.

"A drop," Macsen said, and Bran waited for the pain, but like before there was no pain. Like before, there was only a thread of pleasure that wound through his veins until it stumbled into the fire at the center of his being. It was more than a drop that Macsen took from him, but far less than he had taken the first night they had slept together. Macsen's hands on him changed, warmed, turned from ice to fire, and Bran gasped and clutched at Macsen's shoulders until he lifted his mouth away from Bran's throat.

Macsen stared at him with eyes full of glow.

"You will be mine forever, Bran Fionnan. You will sleep in my bed, live in my chambers — you will be more than just my lover. We'll attend the great dances, and I'll teach you the flavor of Winter. I'll bring you beyond the edges of my kingdom, to the Summer palace where you were born, to dark festivals under the Black King's reign. Then we'll return to the moonlight and the dark, or we'll go out among mortals and you will ride beside me in the Hunt."

Macsen pushed himself back and sat up on his knees over Bran's thighs. He traced a scar as he drew his fingers down to Bran's hips. A thin line of ridged flesh wrapped from the top of Bran's buttock around his side, toward his navel. Bran remembered it well, the long, narrow remnant of an old wound.

"Where did this scar come from, Bran of mine? It's old, not from—"

Macsen cut himself off, and Bran stopped smiling.

"It was a reminder. The only one I was allowed or even given, my first and only lesson on what it meant to disobey the Milesians or their king.

"The next time I disobeyed, I would die. If I was useless to them, would not obey, why should they keep me? That's what he said. I wondered, too—what the point of staying alive was. But..."

Bran shrugged.

"I guess Mac Briuin kept his word. Anyway, I'm here now."

Macsen's expression gained a layer of darkness that disturbed him.

"Only revenge can correct something like that, Bran of mine."

Bran sat up and Macsen tumbled off his body. Macsen scowled from beside Bran on the bed, and more when Bran spoke.

"No, Macsen. I don't want any more revenge. It's enough for me to be here—to be here with you, if you'll have me."

"Have you! Haven't you been listening to me, Bran Fionnan? I will never let you go. But that woman we left behind, that huntress—"

"Dealla."

"Yes, that one."

"Trained to be what she was, just like Noirine and many others. Protecting humans from your kind—our kind—it's their nature, just like the blood thirst that's *your* nature."

Bran closed his eyes.

"I can't stop you. I know it. But I've at least learned enough about love to know that if you *do* love me you won't go after them."

Macsen stood and looked down at him from the end of the bed. "You want nothing from them? Nothing to repay what they did to you?"

Bran shook his head. "No, I want nothing *else*. You killed their king, Macsen, set your Hunt loose on them, and now the Summer *sidhe* — my people won't abide by the old pact, will they?"

Macsen grinned, and the expression was full of hunger and promise and glee. "No, they won't. But that wasn't really my doing. The barrows have been open since the moment the Milesians crossed into your mother's realm with dark intentions. I just made Summer's people aware of that fact. No matter what I do — or you ask — the Milesians will have trouble with your mother's people even if I don't send the Red Court after them."

Bran said nothing. He waited with his eyes on Macsen until Macsen sighed and glared at him.

"This one thing, I'll give to you just because you ask it. No more revenge, no more death than is in my nature. I will not send the Wild Hunt to torment them again, I'll stay to my own territory. But Bran — remember. Macsen Cadoc can grant you that boon, but the Red King will only swear by it as long as those fools stay where they belong."

The end of one world and the beginning of another came to Bran with that promise. So dangerous, this moment! But oh, therefore — forever — becoming — *perfect*.

"We are back at the beginning now, Bran Fionnan. Everything you want, I've given you. What else do I need to do to make you admit you love me?"

Bran blinked and tried to wipe all his desires from his thoughts, tried to think rationally, but the only words that came to him were the words Macsen wanted, the words he himself feared. *Macsen Cadoc, I love you.*

"I want you closer than my skin, I want you for my truth, Bran."

"*Yes—*"

The word slipped out of Bran's mouth before he could contain it. It was an answer to Macsen and to his own thoughts.

Macsen spoke again, his words intent and serious.

"I will claim from you whatever is your soul, all that promise and light. I will consume it like the beating hearts offered to ancient gods, and give you myself in return. Do you accept the exchange, Bran Fionnan? I won't give up what I take for my own."

The words were old and lovely and heavy with promise. It was an ancient vow, offered unaltered in form but with sharper meaning. It carried the echo of Macsen's first promise along with something new.

This was the one who wanted him and who he wanted, the one who had claimed him, endangered him, the one who had slain a king to save him. Macsen's last statement rang in Bran's head, blatant in its promise—a promise, Bran thought, that he wanted more than anything else.

'I won't give up what I claim for my own.'

"I'll be yours just as much as you are mine, Macsen Cadoc."

Macsen looked up at Bran with burning tension at the center of his being.

"Submit *now*, Bran Fionnan. You must give in, sunlight to shadow."

Bran laughed and reached out to push Macsen's hair back from his face. His fingers lingered. Macsen rose up and kissed him, and in a moment had their positions reversed, had Bran pressed down against the bed with the weight of his body "Your submission, Bran Fionnan. You said *yes* to me, just now. Is your memory as bad as that?"

Bran scowled, but Macsen wasn't through yet.

"Did I not submit to you? Have I not given you what you wanted, what you demanded from me?"

"I already gave you *everything* — "

"*No*. It is not your body that concerns me, Bran, but everything else."

With the fingers of one hand he stroked Bran's chest. He kept Bran still with the other, held his arms at the wrist and leaned forward over him.

"Beautiful Bran, tell me you love me."

He considered threatening Bran with the vengeance he had promised not to take and rejected the idea. He had given his word — even if Bran still objected! He knew that the feeling was there, but he wanted it acknowledged, wanted it in the open — just knowing Bran desired him wasn't enough!

Bran closed his eyes for a single moment, and Macsen heard a desperate murmur escape his lips.

"I could lie, if only it wasn't true."

"You can't escape me, Bran."

Bran opened his eyes. "Yes — and you know I won't fight you, I want you too much, I told you that...at the beginning."

"But you won't say those words, won't tell me that you love me."

"I shouldn't have to tell you, you should know already that I — do."

Macsen bruised Bran's lips with the intensity of his kiss, the heat of it. For a moment they were only bodies again, moving together, wanting together, but Macsen was in control, had to be in control—had to have this one, this only thing. Only the words would be the truth, only the words. Bran couldn't lie to him now, but what if tomorrow—the endless tomorrow— he could?

"Say it—say it now, Bran Fionnan!"

His voice compelled, or maybe his kiss. He tasted Bran, sunlight and honey, gold and blood.

"I love you." The words slipped hoarse and husky from Bran's mouth, so quiet that Macsen thought at first it was an accident. Then Bran said it again, louder—certain, this time.

"I love you."

* * * *

Bran arched up from the bed despite Macsen's hold on him and took the kiss he had been desperate for since the beginning, took the kiss that had been waiting ever since Macsen had first appeared at Bran's threshold, a stranger. Bran's feeling, given words, was not greater now but seemed so, was not different now but filled him with an entirely different heat.

He'd been alone, always alone. He had rarely *considered* love, but feeling it now, knowing it now, he knew it was the thing he'd been missing more than anything else his whole life. And it was his now—and Macsen was his—

Bran sank back against the bed beneath Macsen's weight, and Macsen's tongue lavished promise against his mouth. Bran learned the shape of Macsen's lips to keep forever, the smooth curve of them, the quirk to the left that was humor and violence both. He tasted Macsen's blood, the red chill of it, from the lip that Macsen cut on purpose. He tasted love in the fire, and love in the copper, love in the bitter and the sweet.

They pulled apart, but only for a moment.

"Tell me again, Bran Fionnan—"

Bran panted the words, "I love you—"

Macsen's mouth moved against Bran's his mouth, against his chest, back to his cheek, up to the curve of his neck and the pounding pulse it hid, then over one shoulder as he wrestled against the strength that held him still. Macsen would have none of it.

"*Again.*"

"I love you."

Macsen sat back then and moved to one side. He reached out and snagged Bran's waist before he had a chance to move too far away, and Bran rolled over and made himself comfortable against Macsen's side. Bran reached out a leg and hooked it around one of his, draped an arm across his body and let the other curl near Macsen's head. Macsen stroked Bran's arm with idle fingers, the ticklish part of his side that woke a shiver in Bran's skin, across the golden down on his chest and back again. Bran nuzzled him, cheek to chest, and yawned, but pleased as he was, Macsen knew they couldn't stay this way for long.

The sun would never rise, not here—but the day was beginning all the same. Macsen scowled. The court held no interest for him, but perhaps now it wouldn't be the same as always. There would be stories, the tale of the Hunt just past, and in the dance tonight he wouldn't be alone, for the first time in forever. Tonight, he would have a true partner.

Macsen reached down and tipped Bran's face up, stroked Bran's cheek with his thumb until those blue eyes were focused on him, then he grinned.

"Come with me now, Bran. The night is new, but it is old and endless. So too is the dance that waits for us. It's time for me to introduce you to my people, time for me to tell them that I no longer rule over them alone."

Bran nudged Macsen's hand away with his cheek and lay back down.

"Later."

Macsen stared down at the top of Bran's head and waited, but nothing else was forthcoming.

"Bran Fionnan —"

"I'm not moving."

Bran's arm tightened around Macsen's waist. "I can't dance, anyway."

Macsen moved cooling fingers against Bran's back, traced aimless, feather-light patterns on his skin. Bran tried to shrug him off, but Macsen only smiled and shifted his touch lower, toward the middle of Bran's back where he couldn't avoid or escape it.

"You slept enough in the mist! Come, now. The dance wants you, beautiful Bran."

Bran yawned again and scowled in Macsen's direction without opening his eyes.

"I already said I can't —"

"You *can*. This dance is in your blood."

Macsen moved his arm out from behind Bran and lifted the other that had been laid across him, kissed the inside of Bran's wrist and tugged at Bran's hand as he stood.

"Come with me! It's time the Winter Court met you — time you met them. Didn't I promise you the night beneath the hill? Come!"

That summoning, it seemed, Bran could not resist, but he still grumbled.

"All right! Fine—just—fine..."

Macsen dressed in red and silver and dressed Bran in selkie-silk, blue the shade of the sea and blue like the twilight shadow of his eyes. Fingertips tingling, he bound a golden circlet about Bran's brow, then pulled Bran behind him, down through his palace to the court.

* * * *

The night outside the palace was more enchanted than Bran had expected. The air was sharp with chill and a faint, pale snow was falling. A thousand fires and a thousand lights drifted through the night, and among them wove strange shadows, some human-shaped and some distinctly not.

Macsen pushed him forward, until Bran was among the dancers. The circle moved outward until the whirling, pounding steps included him. Bran turned and found Macsen spinning behind him. He could see no drums, but he heard them, felt their vibrations in his feet—no flutes but he heard those too, high arcs of wailing sound.

The dance was timeless. Eternal or momentary, it made no difference, but Bran felt the moment when it was over and drew himself out of the circle. He felt Macsen behind him, beside him, and whispers settled around him.

"So this is the one that belongs to our King—"

"What a Hunt that must have been!"

From behind Bran, Macsen's voice rang out sudden and sharp. It cut through the sound of invisible music, and the multitude of forms and colors grew silent and turned to face him.

"I am Macsen Cadoc, dark Winter's king—the Red King! Today I come to tell you that I will no longer rule alone. The one I have chosen stands before you. Bran Fionnan, my consort. My lover—my soul."

Bran looked around him and saw then the true faces of the fae, revealed here where they were most themselves. He saw beauty that was too beautiful and became ugliness, and ugliness that was so ugly it had become perfect and was beauty. There were tall, thin women with carapaces of jewels like fine chitin from some glittering insect and striding, enormous dimnesses that carried weight in their presence. There were shapes like himself and Macsen too, males and females in flesh too rich for mortal burdens.

It was one of these who came forward first, a lady whose presence was bright and raw. Her hair and eyes were the color of honey, and her skin was the green gold hue of summer's ripeness. She held out her hands to Bran, and he took them. Her grasp was light and her fingers were long and warm. Her eyes searched his face for a long moment, before she let go of his hands, took two steps back and made a slow, deep curtsy.

"You are the one! Today is a day of unexpected joy. Welcome back, Bran Fionnan. I am your mother's emissary to the Red King's court. Whispers said he had found you, our stolen prince, but neither your mother nor I believed them—and yet they are true."

Bran blinked at her, almost confused.

"You're—an emissary?"

The golden lady smiled at him.

"Your mother is the queen of Summer's people, and I do my duty to her."

Bran felt a sudden wariness infect him.

"I know that. But...your duty...you're not trying to take me away from here, are you?"

"No, no. But a message must be sent to her at once, and I should tell her — are you happy?"

Bran's grin was almost an answer by itself.

"Love is more than happiness, lady. Will you — bring a message for me? Tell my mother — tell her — "

A thousand thoughts welled up in him, a thousand feelings, and he knew suddenly that no message could convey anything worthwhile, not unless he had time to organize his thoughts.

"Never mind. I'll come find you, later, when I've had time to think."

The emissary smiled, and revealed a predator's teeth. Bran was not surprised. It seemed to be a truth of the fae that appearances were deceiving — was that not the case with Macsen Cadoc?

The emissary bowed low.

"Thank you, my lord. I — *we* — are at your service."

They all bowed then, all those strange people — Macsen's people, Bran's people — but Bran saw that not everyone was as pleased to do so as the emissary.

There were black stares and a current of whispers that made him think not everyone wished him and Macsen *happiness*. There were questions running through the dim susurration of the crowd, unhappiness and restlessness beneath the smiles.

Behind the ranks of *sidhe* bowed over in respect, a single figure stood upright and waved at him, escaped the hands of someone else and came running, skipping toward him. He recognized the person at a distance, and grinned with relief. *Saoirse Saorla*. She was smiling and looked unhurt, despite what Macsen had told him about her condition when he'd found her. Someone had dressed her in *sidhe* clothes, immortal silk that shone in the moonlight and a cloak of fine, dark fur.

"Bran Fionnan! Bran Fionnan — you're safe now, you're all better!"

Saoirse flung herself at him, squeezed tight and almost knocked Bran to the ground. He wrapped his arms around her for a moment then held her back at arm's length, crouched and looked into her face.

"I am. I am better, and you? Are you happy? I would have asked you first if I could, before I sent Macsen for you, but I don't think it was safe for you there."

"I'm very happy! The Red King stole me, and Talaith has been watching me and there are many people here who like me, it's not like home at all. And I saved your staff, I brought it with me, because the Red King — oh!"

She stepped back from Bran's grasp and looked up at Macsen, and Bran snickered under his breath at the expression that momentarily passed over the Red King's face. Perhaps he thought Saoirse was going to jump at him, too? Bran wouldn't have been surprised if she did, but the girl curtsied low instead.

"Thank you for saving me, Red King."

Macsen stared at her for a moment then at Bran. Bran could only shrug, holding back laughter, and Macsen finally nodded at the girl.

"You are welcome — but go back to Talaith now, Saoirse Saorla. There will be time for…visiting…later."

The girl grinned and turned back the way she had come. Bran watched Saoirse run back through the muttering *sidhe*, then turned and saw Macsen climb up to his throne and lounge there, his posture bored and careless, his expression anything but. Beside the Red

King's throne of frost and shadow, another was becoming, one of far less frost and far more light.

"Aren't you going to come sit beside me, beautiful Bran?"

"Of course. I wouldn't want someone else to take my place."

The words were a joke, but Macsen's answer was serious.

"That will never happen. I already told you, I won't give up what I take for my own. You are mine, Bran Fionnan."

Bran mounted the steps and sat carefully, but found his seat neither cold nor insubstantial. *Magic.*

"Yes," Bran said. Then, almost an afterthought, "You're mine too, Macsen Cadoc."

The music resumed, and the impossible whirl of the *sidhe* in their dance. Macsen reached across the narrow space that separated him from Bran and drew him close, claimed a smug, swift kiss.

"Of course I am. I always get what I want."

Bran's laughter rang, gold as bells above the throbbing drums.

Epilogue

Days had passed since the night Dealla would forever remember as the end of the world. There had been fighting and terror for a day and a night after Imbolc, confusion in the forests and the villages, panic wherever men had made their homes...but since then, there had only been silence. *Too much silence.*

Invisible presences were returning to the land that had been empty for a thousand years. Snowy hills and ice-threaded brambles were full of rustling and murmurs. Flowers blossomed out of season, and trees thought long dead sprouted green leaves. The winter quiet was now an *un*quiet, a deep and waiting silence. For what, she didn't know.

Not for summer, that much was obvious. The *sidhe* could make summer where and when they chose. For the Red King? Yet why would Summer's people wait for him? He had only come and gone, taken what he wanted and left.

Bran Fionnan.

The name echoed in her thoughts, sudden and clear. How she despised that name! She would hate it until she died, and after— Since the first time, whenever she heard it, whenever she spoke it, she held the loathing of it in her mouth like a burning coal for hours afterward. More than the Red King did she detest Bran Fionnan. He had been her prisoner—he had been too weak to move, and still he had been responsible for the end of the world!

The Red King would never have come if not for him. *Bran Fionnan.*

Dealla was jerked out of vengeful thoughts by the sounds of horse hooves on hard earth, loud male voices speaking in earnest. The door to the great hall, shattered by the Red King, had yet to be repaired, and the noise from outside was carried sharp and clear to her ears by a cold wind.

"They're here."

Dealla rose from her father's throne—*my throne, now. My throne, not his*—and fixed her most imperious expression to her face.

When her *guest* walked over the threshold a few moments later, she greeted him with the words she had prepared—cutting, accusatory.

"Well, druid, what have you to say? The whole of my land has been ravaged. My father's blood, a king's blood, was spilled in the dirt like that of a common slave. North to south, sunrise to sunset shore, I am told that there are few places left untouched by the darkness."

She turned her eyes to the druid.

"You, old man. You are Lughaid mac Raghnall, the one who speaks to the gods."

Lughaid the druid had wild white eyebrows, but below them his eyes were mild and blue.

"This is the truth."

She waited for the compulsory genuflection at the end of his words, but he said nothing — no *my lady*, no *my queen* — even if the latter was not precisely true, wouldn't be true until the council approved her coronation... There was something mocking in his gaze that Dealla didn't like, something that simultaneously appraised and dismissed her. She stared at him for a long moment, but he answered her silence with silence and an unwavering stare of his own, eyes bright as a hawk's.

She turned and sat on the throne, stroked the dark, carved wood of the armrests.

"Tell me, druid...why is it that your places were untouched by the darkness? Why is it that the ancient groves remain pristine?"

He laughed.

"That's your question? That's why you called me here? Even a simpleton knows better than to hurt his own household — bird or beast, neither fouls its own nest. So it is with the *sidhe*. They are the children of the ancient gods, the first spirits. The pools and forests, the circles of stone, those are their places, now as they were in the old times. "

Dealla felt a surge of nausea. The old fool sounded delighted!

"Druid, do you understand the trouble that your precious *sidhe* have caused? *You* know the old powers, the ancient words, the omens and auguries, the weaknesses of our enemy. If you do not conspire with them, if you are not an enemy of man — "

She leaned forward on her throne.

"Help me fight against them, so we may keep our land!"

The bird-bright eyes of the druid looked up at her from beneath shaggy white brows.

"*Our land?*"

He laughed again, and Dealla sat straighter, insulted.

"Time was when the world was all misty shadows, all green. Time was when all of it was *theirs*, and the hidden kingdoms only a vanity and a pleasure and a torment to mortals. Not like now, the hidden places becoming all that remain to them..."

Lughaid's voice took on a sad tone that Dealla found irritating.

"Time was when we humans knew our place, just like everything else in the world. Woman, queen that you seek to be, even if I could help you I would not—but my lack saves me the trouble of refusing. There is nothing I can do to aid you in violence. Of the old powers, the old magics, I'm sure you know enough of those to do as you please, but I have no secret of destruction."

Dealla frowned at him.

"Magic is not enough to fight the *sidhe*, and the Red King—

She saw the pale features in her mind's eye, remembered the voice that had stabbed at her ears like a spike of ice.

"Druid, the Red King is the most dangerous creature I have ever encountered."

"And yet he let you live."

"You—"

But her fury was frustrated by the calm face the old man presented to her. She tightened her hands on the arms of the throne, dug her fingernails into the wood.

"Druid, you are a fool if you think that these creatures can be trusted, that there is anything good or worthwhile about them. Can't help, won't help—

either is as bad as the other, and makes you of no use to me. Get out!"

Lughaid stared at her, brows contracted, face frowning, then shook his head and turned away.

Dealla dismissed him from her thoughts. If Lughaid would not help her, perhaps there were others of his ilk who would—men less scrupulous, or more loyal. One way or another, she would have what she wanted. Vengeance for her father and the broken kingdom she would inherit, for the terror and the theft of an ancient peace. She would revenge herself on the Red King, would find some way to hurt him, to *break* him, even if it took all the years of her life.

"And I know just how to do it, don't I?"

She spoke to the shadow and silence of the empty hall.

"You may be invulnerable, *Red King*, but the one you risked so much to save is not. Bran Fionnan..." The name whispered past her lips and she felt it go, clinging and painful as hot grease on old blisters.

About the Author

Belinda currently lives on the New England coast with her fiancée, their room mate and her cat. When she's not writing, she's working toward degrees in Philosophy and English, embroidering or reading.

Belinda writes in several genres, but a little lust and love always work their way into her stories.

Belinda Burke loves to hear from readers. You can find her contact information, website details and author profile page at http://www.totallybound.com.

Totally Bound Publishing

www.ingramcontent.com/pod-product-compliance
Lightning Source LLC
Chambersburg PA
CBHW020433180626
46812CB00003B/1214